FOUR HORSEMEN

Dave Turner

Aim For The Head Books

Aim For The Head Books
149 Long Meadow
Aylesbury, Buckinghamshire, HP21 7EB

www.daveturner.co.uk

ISBN: 9781838381011

ONE

20th December 1874

A black carriage flew over the moonlit cobbled streets. Wheels clattered on stone. The horses strained at their bridles, urged forward by the lash of the driver's whip. Snowflakes stung his face like sharp rocks, but he didn't slow their charge.

An inexplicable excitement hung in the winter air; a feeling the world was on the cusp of change. It forced the driver onwards, faster and faster. He was but a humble coachman. He had no knowledge his passengers' destination would be the setting for an event spoken of only in hushed voices for centuries afterwards. But more of that later.

Inside the carriage, three men (or man-shaped creatures at any rate) in full evening dress were late for a party. He that was known as 'War' gazed out the window at the pedestrians diving out of the way of the thundering hooves.

'It's not natural to travel this way,' he moaned. 'Coddled in a carriage like babies. I'm only really happy when I have a magnificent stallion charging between my thighs.'

Conquest adjusted his white cotton gloves and raised a well-sculpted eyebrow. 'First, that's a powerful image. Second, have you seen the states of the streets out there? I'm not turning up like I've been sleeping in an outhouse.'

'Whose party is it?' War asked as he poked his large, calloused fingers between his neck and well-starched collar. He found the bow tie and tailcoat, and all the manners and behaviours that came with them, more constricting than a suit of armour.

'Archibald Christou,' Conquest replied. War stared at him blankly. Conquest sighed. 'Archibald Christou? Summoned us with ancient spells? Wanted to destroy the world?'

War shrugged. 'That could be one of several people.'

Famine, pale skin pulled tight over the delicate bones of his skull, brushed biscuit crumbs from his trousers. 'You turned up naked with a rubber duck.'

War smiled at the memory. 'Ah, yes. Ducky. A fine friend. What's the occasion?'

Conquest pointed to the decorated shop fronts that flashed by in the glow of the gaslight. 'Christmas?'

'Remember when it was a pagan festival?' Famine asked between bites of biscuit.

'It was a lot less formal,' War said, fidgeting in his seat.

Conquest grinned. 'Yes, I miss the orgies too.'

'Could've done with less human sacrifice, though.'

'Well, they've always had their festive quirks,' Famine said. 'Like Christmas pudding now.'

'What are you eating, anyway?' War asked.

'Garibaldi.'

'Like the Italian fella?'

Famine offered the packet. 'Yes. Do you want one?'

War took a biscuit, eyed it with suspicion and put it back. 'Do they squash the insects in before or after the baking process?'

'They're raisins.'

'Biscuits are more Death's thing,' War said. 'Where is he?'

'Spending eternity ferrying tortured souls to infinite rest,' Conquest said.

War tugged at his collar again and gazed at the night sky. 'Lucky bastard.'

Christou Hall was from the Go-Hard-or-Go-Home School of Architecture. Built on the outskirts of London, it was testament to what could be achieved when the client had ambition, cash and a spectacular amount of opium.

They'd demanded unnecessary turrets and ornate staircases that didn't seem to climb anywhere. Monstrous gargoyles and scenes that Hieronymus Bosch would describe as 'a bit much' were carved into the stone walls. Wildfowl roamed between the fountains and statues scattered around the expensively maintained gardens.

The Three Quarters of the Horsemen of the Apocalypse's carriage swept up the driveway dragging at least one peacock in its wheels. It ground to a halt at the house's entrance, where two giant Christmas trees flanked the heavy wooden door. The

Horsemen stepped down from the carriage, the gravel crunching beneath their feet, and Conquest walked around to the front.

'Thank you very much,' he said, handing a note to the frost-encrusted coachman. Over his shoulder, War leaned on his cane and coughed sharply. Conquest sighed and handed over another note. 'Get the horses something nice.'

'Animal lover, are we?' the coachman asked.

'We used to be in the trade.'

The butler opened the door with a detached smile unaffected by years of ridiculous demands from awful people. He led them through corridors lined with portraits of generations of Christous, whom the three guests had all outlived.

Fashionably late, the party was in full swing when the Horsemen entered the ballroom. Candlelight bathed the scene in an ethereal glow so beautiful that if Instagram existed, you wouldn't need to apply a filter. Dancers waltzed along the edge of the dance floor while a string quartet played. Ladies gossiped and sipped from delicate stemmed glasses while, out of earshot, gentlemen told bawdy jokes.

War looked around anxiously. He was only comfortable in large crowds if one half was trying to beat the other into submission with blunt objects. Give him an angry Celt with a claymore over a society lady making small talk any time.

'If it isn't the three most eligible bachelors in London,' said Archibald Christou as he approached. They all shook hands. War became confused and shook Conquest's. 'I'm so glad you were able to come.'

'Where's the buffet?' Famine asked, all business.

Archibald laughed and pointed to an archway leading to an anteroom. 'Through there, my friend. We have delicacies to delight even a gourmand such as yourself.'

'Thank you.' Famine disappeared like a vol-au-vent-seeking missile.

Archibald turned to Conquest. 'How have you been?'

'Excellent, thank you. How are you?'

'Fine,' Archibald replied with a forced smile. 'Business is booming. I've invested heavily in this new underground railway system. I predict great things from it.'

War laughed. 'It's nothing but a fad.'

'You said that about the wheel,' replied Conquest. He turned back to Archibald, placed a hand on his shoulder. 'How are you, personally?'

'Well, you know, I always find this time of year difficult since Sarah passed away. The world relentlessly grinding on as one year turns into the next.'

'Think of it as punching a hole through time like an angry god. Makes the New Year a bit more exciting,' War said.

'Thank you. I'll try to remember that,' Archibald replied, confused. 'Sarah always loved Christmas.'

War groaned. 'Oh, bloody hell. Not her again.'

'I beg your pardon?' Archibald asked, his face reddening with anger.

'Oh, not you. I was talking about Lady Dotrice,' War pointed to the other side of the hall. 'She's been pursuing me for months.'

A young lady strapped tightly into silk and satin gave a shy smile before turning to her friends and giggling.

Conquest slapped War on the back. 'Ask her to dance. You just need the love of a good woman. Actually, a bad one will probably do.'

'Unlike you, Conquest, I don't have an overwhelming need to bond with humans. They're so fragile. Have you seen how easily their arms come out of their sockets?'

'Yes. You showed me.'

'That was a busy weekend, wasn't it?'

They laughed as Archibald edged away. This was the Victorian Age, and he was unsure of the etiquette when immortal beings discussed dismemberment. 'I think I'll check on Famine. Please, have a drink. Enjoy yourselves.'

TWO

Twas the night before the night before the night before the night before the night before Christmas, when all through the house not a creature was stirring. Apart from the being of unspeakable horror hiding under the bed.

Joseph heard it breathing. He pulled all his limbs beneath the covers because every eight-year-old boy knew the monsters can't get you if no part of your body's exposed. The cold slipped through the window and he saw his own breath; short, staccato gasps like smoke signals of distress.

The weight shifted beneath him as the creature slid out from under the bed. Joseph pulled the blankets over his face and squeezed his eyelids together. He sensed the creature stand up, ancient bones creaking as it unfolded into whatever horrific form it took. He wished it would go away. At this time of year there was only one nocturnal visitor he'd want standing at the foot of his bed.

'Come out from under there, child. Open your eyes. See who's come to visit you.' A kind voice. A voice that wished no harm.

Calmed, Joseph peeled the covers down to his chin and opened one eye. Red trousers and black boots. His gaze drifted upwards. A large belly squeezed into a red jacket and, above that, a jolly face framed by white hair and beard. Joseph opened both eyes in wonder. 'Father Christmas?!'

The jolly face looking down on him grew wider with a grin. 'The very same,' he chortled, ruffling the young boy's hair. Joseph sat up.

'Aren't you early?'

'I suppose I am,' said Father Christmas, 'but you're a special boy, aren't you?'

Joseph looked down at his chilled hands. 'Daddy tells me the only thing special about me is how lazy I am.'

'But you know different, don't you?' Father Christmas asked with a twinkle in his eye. Joseph went to say something, but then held his tongue. 'Go on. I won't tell anybody. If you can't trust Father Christmas, who can you?'

Joseph looked up into his eyes. He knew he could tell him anything. 'I can do something others can't.'

'Can you now?' Father Christmas moved closer, crouching down so his face was level with Joseph's. Joseph nodded.

'I can tell what people are thinking, sometimes. Or feeling. If I concentrate hard enough.'

'Well, that is most interesting. Can you tell what I'm thinking?'

'I can't read Father Christmas's thoughts. What if I learned who's been naughty or nice? I wouldn't like to find out I'm on the naughty list.'

'I shouldn't tell you this, but you're on the nice list. I'd like you to try. Didn't they teach you to do what adults ask?' That was true. Joseph's parents always told him that.

'If you say so.' He screwed his face up in concentration. After a while, his mind slipped loose from his body and travelled the short distance to the man crouched beside him. He tried and tried, his thoughts probing around the edges of the consciousness in front of him, but he couldn't grasp anything. He sat back, hands rubbing his aching head.

'Is something wrong?' Father Christmas asked.

'I can't do it,' Joseph said. 'There's just a big hole there.'

Father Christmas looked at Joseph with a hunger that made him uneasy. 'Oh, but look how it makes you sparkle and shine, like a special festive treat.'

Joseph backed away until the cold wall pressed against his back. 'You're not Father Christmas. Father Christmas has never visited me before. Why would he now?'

'Of course I'm Father Christmas. Look. I've got the beard, the red suit, the jolly laugh,' Father Christmas laughed in a jolly, if forced, manner.

'Did you get my letter?'

'I did.'

'What did I ask for?' The question surprised Father Christmas. Joseph wasn't able to read his mind, but he saw the gears working behind his eyes.

'A cuddly toy.'

'What am I? Six years old?' Joseph replied.

'Yes...?'

'I'm eight years old. I asked for a toy train.'

'All right, Inspector Bloody Bucket. I'm not Father Christmas.' The twinkle returned to his eyes. 'You wanted me to be him so here I am. But I'm something much, much better. And I have a present for you.'

Joseph moved closer, his curiosity aroused. 'Nobody's better than Father Christmas.'

The Not-Father-Christmas reached into his pocket and pulled out a small Christmas bauble. It sparkled and spun in the moonlight and was quite the prettiest thing Joseph had ever seen. He reached out to touch it, but Not-Father-Christmas snatched it away.

'What does your future hold, Joseph?' Joseph shrugged. He couldn't take his eyes off the bauble.

'Father says I have to work in the factories next year. He says we can't afford me staying in school and learning stuff I'll never have a need for.'

'What if I took you to a magnificent place? Somewhere you can be with lots of other boys and girls? You'll never grow old, or work in the factories, or climb up a chimney, or have to do anything you don't want to.'

'I have no friends here. What if I don't make any there?'

'Oh, but they're all as special as you are. They're all dying to meet you.' Joseph nodded dumbly. It sounded wonderful. Much better than the future he'd resigned himself to. 'Well, then. This is yours.'

Not-Father-Christmas placed the bauble into Joseph's open palm. The skin underneath the glass globe tingled and grew cold. A numbness flowed up his arm and across his chest. His breath quickened with the shock of the chill. He looked up at Not-Father-Christmas, his eyes wide with panic. Not-Father-Christmas leaned closer, his welcoming grin now just a memory.

'Never bargain with the monster hiding under your bed,' he hissed.

The bauble swallowed the boy up and dropped onto the empty blankets. Not-Father-Christmas picked it up. He blew gently making it dance and twirl, the bright facets reflecting in his large eyes.

'Welcome to the Other Place, boy.'

THREE

Famine examined the bounty spread before him. Roasted meats, delicate pastries, sweet desserts and exotic fruits. The Buffet of the Gods.

He picked at a plate of canapés before turning his attention to the different parts of innumerable animals. When finished with them, he moved onto the cheese and biscuits, but soon abandoned the biscuits as they were just slowing him down. Archibald appeared at his shoulder.

'I hope you're finding our modest offering to your satisfaction?' Famine mumbled his approval through a mouthful of cheddar. Archibald offered him a plate filled with cubes of a strange yellow fruit. 'Have you tried the pineapple? I've had it imported for this evening.'

Famine took a slick cube and popped it into his mouth. His eyes lit up when the pineapple hit the cheese and the combination exploded in the mouth. Thunder and lightning rolled across the heavens outside. The skies were clear, but thunder and lightning tended to roll wherever the Horsemen were. It suited the occasion. These were momentous times. A legend was about to be born.

Famine picked up a cube of cheese and pressed it together with a pineapple chunk. He held it to

Archibald's lips. 'You must try this.' Archibald protested until Famine said, 'I must insist, Mr Christou.'

Archibald looked at the food with suspicion before taking it with one bite. His eyes grew wider as he chewed, savouring the flavour igniting his taste buds. He reluctantly swallowed, not wanting the moment to end.

'When I invited you to my home tonight, I had little idea I would taste the divine. Thank you, sir.'

Famine grabbed Archibald by the shoulder. 'We must make more.'

'There must be a way of binding them together.' They both thought for a moment.

'Cocktail sticks!'

As Famine cut more cubes of cheese, Archibald summoned a servant. 'Bring me cocktails sticks.'

'How many would you like, sir?'

'As many as you can muster. Go now, man!'

When the servant returned, Famine and Archibald speared the cubes; cheese on top of pineapple, pineapple crushed against cheese. It was a finger food massacre.

'They need to be presented with style,' Archibald said.

Famine looked around the table until his eyes landed on a grapefruit. He grabbed a knife and sliced it in two. Then they pressed the cocktail sticks into one half until it resembled a cheesy, fruity hedgehog. Famine held a cheese and pineapple stick to the light.

'I shall call it the Christou, in honour of he who allowed this creation to exist.' He bit into it, sliding the stick out from between his teeth. 'Let it be known, from this day forward, that a party is but a mere gathering if these cheese and pineapple sticks do not adorn a buffet table.'

And even though the name would be lost to history, the British would obey Famine's proclamation for years to come whenever they came together in celebration.

In a catastrophic tactical error, War found himself cornered by Lady Dotrice.

'Tell me, Mr Warfield. Such an unusual name. From where do you hail?' she asked, fluttering her eyelids. War wondered if it was particularly dusty in the ballroom.

'I was born from Chaos and Pandemonium,' he replied, trying to plan an exit strategy.

'Really? I adore Scotland.'

As War looked for a way out of the conversation, he noticed three new arrivals. He sensed trouble from their demeanour. Their leader, a man of high status planning low deeds, scanned the room until he found who he was looking for; Conquest, regaling a captivated crowd with stories.

'You must excuse me,' War said to Lady Dotrice.

Famine appeared waving what looked like cubes of wax impaled on a small skewer. 'You must try one,' he said to War. War watched the trio march with purpose across the dance floor towards Conquest.

'Not now,' he replied. ' I think our friend needs our help.'

Famine wiggled the stick under War's nose. 'I shall not rest until you've tried one.'

War sighed. 'Fine,' he said, snatching the cocktail stick from Famine's hand. He almost bit through the wood as he chomped down. 'Good God, Sir, What sorcery is this? It's like there's a celebration in my mouth and everybody's drinking sunshine and moonbeams!' He shook Famine by the shoulders. 'Tell me we have more!'

'A veritable feast.'

'Then once we have dealt with whatever trouble Conquest has gotten himself into, we shall dine like kings!'

War turned to Lady Dotrice and bowed. 'My lady.'

She blushed and fluttered her eyelids. 'Mr Warfield.'

Conquest had reached the punch line of a particularly good joke when he felt a finger tap his shoulder. While his audience laughed, he turned to see who the finger was attached to. The absence of chin and haughty expression on the face he stared into told of an aristocratic heritage.

'Can I help you?' asked Conquest, already sizing up the other gentlemen stood two paces back.

He noticed the glove too late, and it smacked him sharply across the cheek. Onlookers gasped as he staggered back from the shock of the blow.

'William Conway?' his attacker asked. Conquest rubbed the red mark on the side of his face.

'Who's asking?'

'I, sir, am Lord Robin De La Croix,' said Lord Robin De La Croix, who was visibly trembling with rage. 'You have wronged me.'

Famine and War joined Conquest, flanking him on either side. To the room's horror, War slid a hidden blade out from his cane and held it to De La Croix's throat in one swift movement.

'What are you doing that for?' Conquest asked.

War nodded towards De La Croix. 'Well, y'know. He slapped you.'

'Put it away!' War lowered his sword. Conquest sighed. 'This is why we don't get invited to nice places.' Conquest turned back to De La Croix. 'And how, sir, have I wronged you?'

'You took advantage of my wife, Lady Isabella De La Croix, in her chamber.' Another gasp from the guests that had gathered around. A few ladies looked in danger of swooning. Conquest scrunched his face up in concentration as he tried to put a face to the name.

'Is she a blonde?'

'No, sir!'

'Brunette?' De La Croix had turned a worrying shade of scarlet.

'No!'

'Redhead?'

'Finally!' Conquest caught Famine's attention and shrugged. Famine rolled his eyes.

'I demand satisfaction!' De La Croix barked.

'So did your wife, apparently,' War said with a grin.

'You're not helping matters,' said Conquest.

'I challenge you to a duel!' De La Croix spat. A third gasp. Conquest was surprised there was still any air left in the room.

'Duelling hasn't been legal for quarter of a century. I don't think it's a good idea.'

'A coward as well as an adulterer?'

Conquest winked at a pretty young thing in the crowd. 'I always said I was a lover not a fighter.' War couldn't abide Conquest's showboating at moments like this.

'Just get on with it,' he said.

De La Croix laid down his challenge. 'I shall meet you on the Heath at dawn tomorrow.'

Conquest groaned. 'Hampstead? That's the other side of town. Do you know how difficult it is to get there at that time of the morning?'

'I'm sorry the matter of my wife's honour is such an inconvenience to you.'

Conquest threw his hands up. 'Fine. Hampstead Heath at dawn tomorrow.'

'Until then,' De La Croix said, pleased with the outcome. 'When we shall settle this matter like gentlemen.' He spun on his heel and led his two silent goons away.

'Lovely to meet you,' Famine called after him.

'Well, he was a delightful fellow,' War said, the words dripping with sarcasm.

'Duel in the morning?' said Famine. 'Probably shouldn't drink any more tonight.'

'Nonsense. I can have a couple.'

War put his arm around Conquest's shoulders. 'In the meantime, come with us to the buffet. We have a wonder to show you.'

FOUR

London was a city of many layers. At the top sat those with wealth, privilege and power. The lowest lived in filth, crime and squalor, surviving in the cracks and shadows, ignored and squeezed on all sides. The guests at Archibald Christou's party would never know such hardship, though they rubbed shoulders with it every day.

Elizabeth Buckingham existed somewhere near the bottom, sandwiched between destitution and the workhouse. While Conquest, War and Famine celebrated the season, she sat on the street, a begging bowl in front of her crossed legs. Two blue eyes beamed from a dirt-smeared face framed by matted curls. She was eight years old though a short lifetime of poor diet and choking city air meant she looked a lot smaller.

Tipping the bowl with a finger, she looked at her takings for the day. A few pennies and a button. She'd need more than that, but the crowds were thinning. It was getting late and it wouldn't be wise to stay on the streets in this part of town. She'd tried the good and honest approach, but now drastic measures were needed. She poured the contents of the bowl into her dress pocket, keeping the button (because you never knew when a spare might be useful), and headed south.

When Elizabeth found the ideal spot; an intersection of two busy thoroughfares, she burst into tears. Heartfelt enough to raise an adult's concern, but not so hysterical to make anyone feel uncomfortable. Soon enough, she caught the attention of an elderly gentleman.

'What's the matter, my dear?' he asked. Elizabeth sized him up, examining the cut and quality of his clothing. Not as wealthy as she'd like, but he'd do.

'I'm lost,' she replied, wiping her wet cheeks with a grubby sleeve in a masterclass of wretchedness. 'I'm trying to find Roth Street. I must run an errand and if I don't get there soon, I'll be in so much trouble with my father.' The gentleman looked into her sad eyes. A mistake on his part.

'Yes.' He pointed to the way he'd just come. 'It's just down there and... and... err... '

The gentleman stuttered to a halt, as if he'd clumsily let the knowledge slip from his head and drop to the pavement. His thoughts were slowing, the gears of his mind gumming up and gluing together, until they came to a dead stop. He stood frozen, an unthinking rabbit caught in headlights. The pedestrians moved around him, oblivious to his helplessness.

Elizabeth carefully detached the pocket watch from his waistcoat and extracted the wallet from the inside pocket of his coat. She tucked both of them away in her own pockets and touched his hand. Like a wind-up toy, the gentleman sprang into life.

'--Turn left and then it's the second right,' he continued, as if nothing had happened.

'Thank you, sir. You're so kind,' Elizabeth said with a smile. He tipped his hat. 'No problem at all, young lady. Now, you run along now.'

So she did.

FIVE

Julie Park's mother had been keen she learned a trade. While a noble ambition, Julie felt it more pragmatic to let other people learn a trade and then give her the money. She became an abstractionist and leather worker from an early age - pickpocket to the layman - and worked the streets of London. It was a decent enough way of living. She chose her own hours and got plenty of fresh air.

Then her sister - the good one - had died, leaving her young daughter Elizabeth an orphan. Julie believed that children were the future (or, at least, her future - what with not being as nimble as she used to be), so she took Elizabeth in.

Julie gave her food and shelter, and kept her out of the workhouse, and in return Elizabeth brought back a supply of pocket watches, wallets and purses. A simple business arrangement that suited all parties (apart from the former owners of the pocket watches, wallets and purses). Still, it was their fault if they didn't pay enough attention to the whereabouts of their possessions. This was London. What did they expect?

Elizabeth was a natural. Her trickery was so subtle, her patter so smooth, it was as if she had a sixth sense. The only thing holding her back was the inconvenient moral issues she had with the whole enterprise, but her need to eat soon won over her need to do the right thing.

Julie fried sausages on a small stove in the back room of the hovel where they lived. The walls were black with filth and smoke. Aside from a card table and a handful of pewter pots, it lacked the home comforts Elizabeth dreamed of as she slept on a rough bed made of old sacking. She didn't dare ask Julie if she'd consider improving their conditions. There were profit margins to think of.

Elizabeth slipped through the dirt-encrusted window set high into the back wall, followed by a blast of winter air. She dropped to the floor, as graceful as a cat, and pulled the window shut.

'Make sure that window's locked. You never know what unsavoury sorts are out there.' Julie laughed wheezily at her own joke. The laugh turned into a cough that rattled around her thin body until she bent double, arms wrapped around her chest. When the coughing subsided, she wiped the blood from her chin with a dirty sleeve. The infection was getting worse and the cold weather didn't help.

'How did it go?' she asked, her voice cracking.

Elizabeth went straight to the warmth of the stove, rubbing her tiny hands together in the flame's glow.

'S'all right,' she said through frozen, chapped lips.

'Got anything for me?'

Elizabeth sighed, emptied the leather and gold from her frayed pockets and dumped them onto the card table. Julie picked her way through the haul with an inquisitive finger.

'Not bad,' she said, examining the exquisitely filigreed timepiece. Elizabeth wiped her frozen nose with the back of her hand.

'It's the most wonderful time of the year, ain't it?'

Julie snapped the watchcase closed. 'Lovely stuff,' she said, picking up the frying pan. 'Sausage?'

SIX

Elizabeth woke with a start. Though sweat soaked her nightgown, she shivered beneath the rough blanket. She'd dreamed of the monster again. There'd been a small boy, about her age, asleep in a cheap wooden bed. She'd seen through his eyes, felt the wonder turn to cold dread as the monster snatched him away. It seemed so real, but monsters didn't exist. 'There are already enough terrible things in this world', her aunt had said when Elizabeth had described earlier dreams.

A book lay on the thin pillow next to her, its spine bent backwards. The candle at her bedside had burnt down. She must have dozed off. There'd be trouble over the wasted wax. She'd been so tired, the exhaustion buried deep into her bones with the cold, but reading was her only escape; worlds her imagination rendered so real that she sometimes thought she might step into the pages.

Elizabeth was a bright girl. She understood that life was hard and thankless. No monsters, but no unicorns or Prince Charming either. She'd been put to work from an early age, to earn her keep, and told she should be grateful to have a roof over her head, trapped in the underclass of London.

But Elizabeth was different. She could do things the other children couldn't. The way she had put the man on the street into a trance, or the way she'd thrown Billy Woods across the road without touching him when he'd been rude. Now, instead of teasing her, the neighbourhood kids simply feared and avoided her. She didn't know which was worse, so she kept her gifts a secret.

Elizabeth could barely remember her parents, but knew she had her mother's eyes. Aunt Julie loved her in her own way. They shared the only bedroom and Julie would allow Elizabeth to crawl into her bed when the dreams were particularly bad, but it wasn't the same as the dimly-recalled comfort of her mother's arms.

She smacked her dry mouth. She needed a glass of water, but the jug by her bedside was empty. Now she had shaken off the fog of sleep, she wondered why. Aunt Julie always brought a fresh jug with her to bed and wouldn't ever let the candle burn down.

Elizabeth glanced over to Julie's unoccupied bed. She slipped out of her own, gasping as her feet touched the cold wooden floor, and padded over to the half-open door.

SEVEN

Death does not stop. Death does not rest. Death does not put his feet up with a good book and a glass of wine as a reward for a job well done. There is no respite from his thankless task. He is the ever-working ferryman and the border between this world and the next is never closed. Sooner or later, he will arrive at everyone's door. All of humanity will look him in the eye.

Tonight, it was the turn of Julie Parks, a young woman still bleary-eyed from the sleep she would never wake from. The ramshackle furniture and bare wooden floor of her home was evidence that hers had been a pauper's existence, but it was not Death's place to judge the quality of the life led.

'Are you the Ghost of Christmas Yet to Come?' she asked, rubbing her eyes with the ball of her hand. Death sighed. This always happened this time of year. He'd given Dickens a piece of his mind when their paths had crossed a while before.

'I'm afraid not, Julie,' he replied. 'Unfortunately, there will not be any more Christmases for you.'

Julie looked down at her own body, now an empty shell lying on the floor. A sob caught in her throat. She remembered falling there, choking, drowning on dry land, her lungs full of fluid. Her vision had darkened, the shadows consuming the light, until her body embraced the darkness and her last thin breath slipped from her lips.

She surprised herself with her next question. Funny what you think of when thoughts are no longer tied to the material world. 'What about Elizabeth?'

'What about her?' Death asked with a shrug. He didn't know who Elizabeth was. Those left behind did not concern him.

'She's my niece. I'm all she's got. If I'm not here, they'll put her in the workhouse.' Death knew of the workhouse. He was a frequent visitor.

'I'm sorry, but there's nothing I can do.' Death straddled two worlds, and those worlds should be kept separate. The dead moved on, the living continued along the path the universe had mapped out for them. He did not get involved with either and if they tangled up with each other, everything became very complicated.

'Aunt Julie?'

A small girl stood halfway up the rickety stairs leading to the top floor of the small house. She ran the rest of the way down and over to the prone body. 'Aunt Julie?' she repeated, shaking the corpse's shoulder.

'Lizzie!' Julie's ghost shouted. 'I'm over here, Lizzie!'

Elizabeth couldn't hear the ghost calling out her name, nor see her stood just a few feet away.

With no response from the body on the floor, she looked vainly for help. Her eyes rested upon Death.

'My name's Elizabeth. Who are you?'

'Bugger,' Death muttered. Everything was about to become very complicated.

'Tell, 'im, Lizzie. Tell 'im I'm all you got,' Julie pleaded.

All Elizabeth saw of Aunt Julie was her cold, still body. She could see Death, though, and she looked him straight in the eyes.

EIGHT

Dawn's thin watery light fell on the frozen heath as if the sun was really unhappy with the whole thing and could really do with an extra twenty minutes. De La Croix and his second, Jarvis, stood on the duelling ground of Hampstead surrounded by a thick curtain of fog clinging to the grassland, reducing the skeletal trees that surrounded them to faded sketches.

The two men stamped their feet and blew into cupped hands to keep the cold from burying deep into their bones. De La Croix checked the time on the pocket watch he'd teased out from deep below thick layers of clothes. His opponent was late; another insult to throw on the pile of indignities.

De La Croix loathed William Conway's kind. New money. No respect for how things should be done. He didn't know his place. Ideas above his station. De La Croix could hear the rumble of hooves and wheels growing louder like an approaching storm. A horse and carriage rattled through the fog at a foolish speed. They ground to a halt, ripping sods of earth and grass up and leaving thick brown tracks deep in the mud.

The coach rocked and shook as the passengers tried to open the door. Just as De La Croix thought the whole carriage was about to tip over on its side, it sprang wide with a final shove and Conquest tumbled out onto the frost-heavy ground. His two reprobate friends staggered out after him, both swigging from brandy bottles. They were all horribly drunk. The red-bearded oaf helped Conquest to his feet and they both attempted to brush the mud and filth from his trousers while giggling like small boys. De La Croix cleared his throat.

'I'm glad you decided to join us, Mr Conway,' he shouted. Conquest looked around for the source of the noise, his head wobbling as if attached to a spring.

'De La Croix! You old bugger!' he slurred when he spotted him. He barrelled over and threw his arms around him, squeezing him in a bear hug. De La Croix tried to wriggle free, gasping for air. Conquest loosened his grip. He'd remembered there was a purpose to this visit. 'So what are we up to?'

De La Croix pulled away and straightened his clothes. He was indignant. 'We, sir, are to settle our differences through force.' Conquest slapped his forehead with such vigour, he almost fell backwards.

'Of course. Apologies. Where do you want me?' He looked at the ground around his feet, arms out, trying to find a suitable place to stand, as if posing for an amusing photograph. De La Croix pushed the anger down to the pit of his stomach and regained his composure. This should be conducted in the correct manner.

'Who do you appoint as your Second?'

'Fellows,' Conquest called over his shoulder. 'Who fancies being a number two?' War and Famine exchanged a glance before sniggering.

'Is this going to take long?' Famine asked. 'I need breakfast. I know a great little place nearby.' War shrugged and passed the bottle he was holding over to Famine.

'I'll do it.'

De La Croix summoned Jarvis by clapping his raw hands together. Jarvis carried a fine mahogany case. He flipped the catches and lifted the lid. War felt a thrill of excitement when he saw the two polished revolvers snug in the velvet lining inside.

'Ooh! Shiny!' Conquest murmured.

'Choose your weapon,' De La Croix ordered.

'The rules clearly state that the method of combat is chosen by the gentleman who has been challenged,' said War.

Conquest waved him away. 'No, no, this is fine. I'm always interested in new methods humans have come up with to destroy themselves more efficiently.' Conquest picked the gun on the left. It weighed heavier than he'd expected. He shifted it in his hand, getting used to the feel of the ivory handle, and waved it at the centre of the clearing. 'Shall we do it over there?'

Conquest led the way followed by War, De La Croix and Jarvis. When they'd reached the designated spot, Conquest attempted to remove his coat. The gun caught in his sleeve and he staggered around as if wrestling a hostile octopus. He disentangled himself and threw the garment in War's direction. He straightened his waistcoat. 'Jolly good. What are the rules here?'

Jarvis took a step forward. 'The two combatants will stand back-to-back. Each will take ten steps away from the other at a walking pace. Once a distance of ten paces has been reached, the combatants may discharge their firearms at their leisure.'

Conquest looked up from examining his gun. 'Sorry, could you repeat that? Everything after "back-to-back".' War grabbed Conquest's shoulders and turned him in the direction he should be facing.

'Walk ten paces that way. Turn. Fire.'

'Understood.' Conquest nodded his head. The nodding became slower and slower until his chin rested on his neck and his eyes closed. War nudged him.

Conquest jerked and snorted, 'I'm awake!'

De La Croix took his position behind Conquest. War could detect the familiar odour of fear. Though the air was freezing, beads of sweat ran down De La Croix's face. His hands shook. He was running through all the standard actions humans performed when death was in proximity.

'Have you been in many duels?' War asked him. De La Croix shook his head. His Adam's apple bobbed as he swallowed. War nodded towards Conquest. 'He has.'

War smirked when he heard a quiet yelp of terror. He took his place next to Jarvis. 'Begin!' he shouted.

Ten paces.

De La Croix took his first hesitant step.

Nine.

They both cocked their guns.

Eight.

Famine found a pork pie in the carriage.

Seven.

Jarvis shifted nervously from one foot to the other.

Six.

War could taste the violence in the air.

Five.

The horse stole the pork pie from Famine's hand.

Four.

The sun broke through the cloud like a warning light.

Three.

Conquest thought about what he'd have for breakfast.

Two.

De La Croix's trembling finger tensed against the trigger.

One.

Famine wondered if it was ever morally justifiable to punch a horse.

Turn.

Conquest's and De La Croix's boots carved the mud as they span round.

Fire.

Gunfire rolled around the heath, startling the birds so they filled the air with beating wings and startled cries. Conquest looked down at the perfect round hole in his shirt. It was positioned directly over his heart.

'Oh, good shot. Well done.' He twirled the gun around his index finger. 'Breakfast, then?'

De La Croix looked from his still smoking gun to Conquest with incredulity. 'Wha... Wha... What?' he stammered.

'You've won. Honour is served and all that, but I've got a full day and I need to be getting on.' Conquest took a step forward to shake hands.

The adrenaline coursing through his veins, De La Croix fired his gun a second time. Another hole punctured the white cotton of Conquest's shirt. Conquest grunted in annoyance.

'I should point out this is a very expensive shirt.' Undeterred, he continued on to congratulate his opponent, who fired all the remaining bullets into his chest.

'Look,' Conquest said calmly. 'I've been very decent about all this but you're not being particularly sporting about your victory.'

'What foul spirits can possess a man that he walks ably with such wounds?' De La Croix asked, his mouth dry and eyes wide in terror.

'I'm bored!' yelled War.

De La Croix drew his sword and charged towards Conquest. He buried the blade in his chest up to the hilt. Conquest fell backwards into the thick mud and lay still. De La Croix laughed hysterically. He looked around with crazed eyes.

'You all saw him. He came for me. It was my duty to expel the demons.'

Conquest pushed himself up onto his elbows. 'This really isn't going to help my hangover.' He stood up, the mud sucking and slurping at his clothes. De La Croix stabbed him again.

'Be gone, wretched fiend!' he screamed. Conquest examined the tattered remains of his shirt.

'Do you earn commission from my tailor or something?'

Another thrust of the blade.

'Right. That's it. I've just about had enough of you. Is this how we're doing it? War, can I borrow your sword?'

'Certainly.' War reached into the carriage and pulled out the sword he kept around in case of emergencies. He threw it over to Conquest, who caught it in one hand. He slid it out of its scabbard, admiring the fine, detailed metalwork that had gone into its construction.

With a Whoomph! the sword ignited with a red flame. De La Croix and Jarvis took one look at the ancient weapon, turned and ran into the fog.

'I'm not entirely sure you should've done that,' Famine said. 'So much for keeping a low profile.'

'How do you turn this thing off?' Conquest asked, turning the sword in his hand. War snatched it back, and the flames died. Conquest pulled his coat back on, buttoning it up to hide the torn shirt. 'I'm sorry, but he was being a bit annoying.'

'Can we get something to eat now?' Famine moaned.

It was at that moment Conquest noticed the coachman staring at his three passengers as if he'd seen the devil himself. 'Don't worry,' he said, 'You'll get a very big tip for this.'

The coachman's expression changed. 'Oh, in that case hop in. Where do you want to go?'

NINE

84 McHoan Gardens had been in the ownership of the same four brothers since its construction in the eighteenth century. It was the most infamous house in London, a city not short of infamy. Though anonymous in design, lurid stories of what went on inside were told from the grandest palace to the lowest slum. It stood tall and broad along most of the length of the street, its flat front set back from the road, and a stone-pillared porch jutted out over the heavy front door.

Though still early morning, the street that ran past it was bustling. Snow had dusted the cobbles and stone. Collars pulled up, rough work wear rubbed against well-cut suits and bowler hats. A taxi carriage pulled up at the kerb and War, Famine and Conquest were deposited on the pavement. Passers-by saw Conquest's mud-caked clothes and gave him a wide berth. After War handed over a large wad of notes, the cab driver snapped the reins and the carriage disappeared into the traffic.

They slipped into the house, closing the front door behind them, and tiptoed across the great hallway leaving muddy footprints behind them.

'Is that you boys?' called a woman from the kitchen at the back of the house.

Conquest winced. Caught in the act. Mrs Burgess, the housekeeper, came out to meet them. She had the hearing of a bat. She folded her arms across her apron.

'And where have you been all night?'

'Party,' War mumbled. Mrs Burgess looked at the dirty tracks that led from the front door.

'What have you done to my lovely clean floor?' She turned her gaze to Conquest. 'Have you been fighting again?'

He stared at the ground, couldn't meet her eyes with his. 'Yes, Mrs Burgess.'

She sighed. 'I don't know what I'm going to do with you boys.'

'The other one started it,' Conquest said petulantly.

'I don't care who started it. You're lucky that Mr Burgess isn't here to hear you talk like that.'

Since Mrs Burgess had turned forty and made her peace with the fact she'd been unable to give her husband the children they both yearned for, she'd taken it upon herself to mother anyone and everyone who entered her world, whether they were the youngest street urchin or centuries-old immortal beings. The Four Horsemen, even Death himself, loved and feared her in equal measure. Sometimes it was hard to tell who was the employer and who was the servant.

She'd worked for the Four Horsemen of the Apocalypse for just shy of ten years. She was shocked when she discovered their true identities, but a job's a job, what with her Steve finding it difficult to hold down gainful employment. Though she was a God-fearing woman and understood their role in the world, they were lovely boys in her eyes. They just needed direction and boundaries, otherwise this sort of thing happened.

She tutted in a way only an Englishwoman could. Conquest was in awe at how such a small sound was able to carry such a heavy load of disappointment and disapproval.

'Your brother is in the library. At least he wasn't gallivanting around town all night with unsavoury types. He says he has something to tell you.' She took a final look at the muddy floor. 'I'm not clearing this up. You know where the bucket and mop are.'

She turned and headed back towards the kitchen. The three Horsemen slouched in the direction of the drawing room entrance.

'And take your shoes off,' Mrs Burgess called over her shoulder.

'Yes, Mrs Burgess,' they answered in unison.

The library of the Four Horsemen of the Apocalypse had no rival in all the British Empire. It was a collection built up over centuries and was central to any home they lived in. Running the length of the house, leather and wood filled each wall from floor to ceiling. First editions included an autographed copy of the Principia Mathematica ('*Alle the Beste, Isaac*') and a Gutenberg Bible with some handwritten suggestions scrawled in the margin of Revelations.

Death casually stood by the roaring fire when Famine, War and Conquest walked in. War threw his sword onto a sofa by the door.

'You'd better move that before Mrs Burgess sees it,' Famine said. 'You know how she feels about weaponry left lying around the house.'

'Hi, lads.' Death tried to lean nonchalantly against the mantelpiece. 'Did you have a good night?'

'What have you been up to?' Conquest asked, his suspicions aroused. Nonchalance did not come easily to Death.

'Elizabeth, I'd like you to meet some friends,' Death said with a sigh. Elizabeth, still in her tatty nightdress, hopped down from an armchair where she had been sitting unnoticed. Nervous, she wandered over and, looking for reassurance in the presence of three strangers, she gripped Death's cloak.

Famine took a step back. 'She's not a little girl ghost, is she?' He was not keen on little girl ghosts; the creepiest of all the supernatural creatures.

'I've told you about bringing your work home with you,' said Conquest.

'She's not dead.' Death pushed her forward. 'Say hello, Elizabeth. You don't have to be frightened. They're your friends too.' She didn't budge, just gripped Death's cloak tighter. He sighed. 'She hasn't spoken a word since we arrived, so I brought her in here and she seemed happy enough reading to herself.'

'Why is she here?' asked Conquest.

'Her mother died last night.'

'And?' said War. 'Lots of children's mothers die but you rarely have the urge to bring home every waif and stray you run into.'

'She could see me.'

'She could see you?' War repeated. 'But you're Death. The whisper on the lips of the damned, the dark companion who walks in the shadows of humanity's souls, the invisible escort of the spirit realm. The living aren't meant to see you.'

'I'm aware of that, but it doesn't change what happened.'

Death slipped in and out of reality as easily as walking from one room to another. When he was on the job, he would exist on the astral plane. There were two reasons for this. First, it was only good manners. Relatives of the recently deceased wouldn't want him hanging around sorting out all the admin that comes with the afterlife. The second reason was psychological. The newly expired had to learn they were no longer part of the world they'd just left behind. This girl saw through the veil to the other side. He couldn't abandon her after she'd looked into his eyes.

'He always gets like this at this time of year,' War observed.

'Get like what?' asked Death.

'Sentimental.'

'They'll send her to the workhouse.'

'We know nothing about raising a child,' said Famine, pragmatic as always.

'How hard can it be?' Death said. 'Food goes in one end and comes out the other. Between those moments you just have to make sure they don't die. Put that flaming sword down please, dear.'

While they argued, Elizabeth had slipped away and found the sword irresistible. She swung it from side-to-side, the flame arcing. War snatched it from her hand and she burst into tears. The Four Horsemen stood in shock, mouths open, like rabbits caught in headlights. How was something so small able to be so loud? They had not one clue between them what to do. Then Conquest had an idea.

'Mrs Burgess!' he yelled at the top of his voice.

Mrs Burgess arrived. 'What's all this racket?' She took one look at Elizabeth's beetroot-red face and turned to her employers. 'What have you been up to?'

'Her mother passed away last night,' Death mumbled into his cloak.

Mrs Burgess knelt down and dried Elizabeth's tears with a handkerchief. Streaks of pink skin were scored through the dirt on her face.

'Oh, you poor thing. I'll run you a nice hot bath and fix you some breakfast. We must get you out of those filthy clothes. These nice men will get you some new ones.'

The Four Horsemen exchanged glances and shrugged, resigned to following her orders, as Mrs Burgess led Elizabeth from the library.

'So, can we keep her?' Death asked.

'She's not a pet,' Conquest replied.

'We can't throw her out onto the street,' Famine said. 'Death's right. She'll just end up in the work-house, or worse.'

'I've been there more times than I'd like.' Death shook his head. 'You wouldn't wish that on any-body. What do you say, War?' War was examining his sword in minute detail, looking for any damage Elizabeth may have caused.

'How did it get so grubby? She held it for literally a second.'

'Do you agree that she can stay?' Famine asked.

'Fine. Whatever. As long as she doesn't touch my stuff.'

'She can stay here until we find somewhere for her to live,' Conquest said. 'Now, does anybody know where we can buy children's clothes?'

TEN

The Burgess's home was an executive hovel in a vibrant neighbourhood with an ever-decreasing number of stabbings and incidents of grave robbery. It featured a popular one up and one down design with a shared outhouse commanding splendid views of the East End of London. With excellent transport links to the factories and slaughterhouses, this was a much sought-after property for the up-and-coming pauper.

Whenever Lynne Burgess made her daily journey home from work, the inequalities that divided London between the rich and the poor were obvious. As she headed east from the bright, clean, bustling roads of Mayfair, the surrounding city grew darker and more intimidating. The buildings hunched over narrow, filthy streets. People bolted themselves behind doors as the sun set behind grimy houses.

Lynne did not fear walking around her neighbourhood at night. These were her people, and she was well-known to them. The street urchins would not touch her. Also, they knew of the blade she carried beneath the heavy fabric of her skirt and the origin of Hopping Clive's nickname.

Her husband, Stephen, crouched over the fire trying to coax the flames with a poker. He turned at the sound of the closing door.

'Those four Big Girl's Blouses keeping you late again?' he asked with a smile.

She kissed him on the forehead and threw her threadbare coat over the back of an empty armchair. She joined him in front of the fire, rubbing her hands in the heat to persuade the blood to return to her fingers.

'Yes, they've got themselves into a bit of a pickle again.'

Stephen rolled his eyes. 'Typical idle rich people with too much time on their hands.'

'You don't know the half of it,' Lynne muttered. Stephen nodded towards the cramped kitchen tucked into the corner.

'Do you want any tea?'

'No, thanks. I ate at work. In fact, the boys insisted I bring some home for you.' Lynne reached deep into her pocket and pulled out a piece of pie wrapped in greaseproof paper. He took it and she could tell he was embarrassed to have spoken ill of them.

Looking back on the day, Lynne thought the Four Horsemen had done as well as could be expected. Judging by the amount of clothes they'd returned with, every garment shop in London had been emptied of their stock. Elizabeth hadn't said a word. At one point, Lynne thought she'd heard her singing, but when she went into the library, she found Elizabeth reading in silence.

Meals were greeted with a small smile of gratitude and, when the sun had set, Lynne put her to bed in one of the many guest bedrooms and sang half-remembered lullabies from her childhood, with the Four Horsemen standing around the bed like honour guards. The little girl drifted off to sleep, carried by the sound of Lynne's voice. Lynne was sure that War had nodded off too.

After tiptoeing out of the room, they'd gathered around the kitchen table and discussed what to do about the problem sleeping on the floor above. Nobody could come up with anything constructive, so Lynne suggested they continue the conversation the next morning and left them to argue amongst themselves.

'I've got something for you.' Lynne could detect a rare nervousness in Stephen's voice. He reached into the inside pocket of his frayed jacket and handed two tickets to her. Lynne read the words embossed on them with amazement. 'We're going to America,' he said.

The words caught in Lynne's throat, jamming up behind one another until they tumbled out in a stream. 'How did you afford these?' Stephen shook his head.

'It's best not to ask.'

'But what about our jobs?'

'We'll find ones when we get there. It's the land of opportunity. New York's streets are paved with gold.'

'Rubbish.'

'Of course it is, but London's are paved with crap so whatever they've got can only be an improvement. It'll be a new start. Open skies and vast land to conquer; not just a squalid corner of a dying, choking city. There's nothing keeping us here. The New World is where our future lies, Lynne.'

Lynne rubbed her hands again. 'Is it warm there?'

'The summers are long and hot and, if we get too cold in winter, then we can find somewhere else. There's room enough.'

'But the boys need me.'

'They're old enough to look after themselves and, if not, they'll just have to find someone else to darn their socks or make sure their soup isn't too hot so they don't burn their tongues.'

Lynne weighed up what kept her here against what waited across the vast ocean. London was in her blood and bones. Her family had lived around here for generations, even before the city had crawled east like a bloated, hungry creature, swallowing the farmlands and marshes that surrounded it. Her ancestors were buried beneath the stone, their remains absorbed into the foundations of the city and washed out into the Thames.

When she thought about what lay across the Atlantic, though, she experienced something she hadn't felt for years. Excitement. Potential. Hope. London stirred none of these things in her anymore and she was certain it wouldn't ever again. All that tied her to the city was memories of the dead. She took Stephen's hands in her own. 'Let's do it.'

ELEVEN

His father's voice. It whispered his name, tugged insistently at the corners of Douglas's dream, until it pulled him up into to the waking world.

Still half asleep, he searched the bedroom. His toys, the rocking horse, the writing desk, were all silhouetted in the pale moonlight. Nothing unusual or out of place. Then, just before his eyes closed, he saw a familiar figure stood in the corner. Douglas sat bolt upright and rubbed his eyes. It was still there. This wasn't a dream.

The figure stepped into the strip of light that slipped through the gap in the heavy curtains. The moustache, the silver hair, the caring eyes creased at the edges...

Papa! He'd come home! Father sat on the edge of the bed and brushed the hair from Douglas's damp eyes.

'Hello, my boy,' he whispered.

'Papa!' Douglas shouted. Papa put a finger to his lips.

'Hush, child. We mustn't wake your mother.'

Douglas threw his arms around his father. 'Does she know you're home? We've both missed you terribly.' Papa winked mischievously.

'I want to surprise her. It's our little secret for the time being.'

Douglas peeled himself from his father and sat back down.

'Where have you been? I had such awful dreams about what had happened.'

'Your dreams tell you the future?' Douglas nodded.

'Yes. They're usually correct, but I'm so glad the ones about you didn't come true. All I wanted was to see you again.'

'You're a special boy. I'm glad I could make your wish come true.'

When father smiled, it seemed slightly out of place, almost imperceptibly twisted and out of shape. Douglas waved the thoughts away. Papa had been gone for a long time. Tiny aspects of his being were bound to change.

'Can I show you something?' Papa asked.

'Yes please.'

Papa held a hand out. 'Come with me?' Douglas hesitated. 'Don't you trust your own father?'

'I do.' Douglas placed his hand in his father's. He felt small as Papa's cold fingers wrapped around it. They crossed the room and Papa took Douglas's dressing gown from the hook on the back of the door.

'You must put this on.' Douglas did as he was told. They slipped out of the room, across the landing and down the stairs. They'd just reached the front door when Carter the butler stepped out of the study. He fumbled for the spectacles tucked into his waistcoat.

'Where are you going to at this time of night, Master Douglas?' he asked, as he adjusted the glasses on his nose. When his vision focused, he looked at the man stood behind the young boy and gasped.

'Young sir, come with me immediately.'

'Papa's back, Carter!' Douglas cried. 'Isn't it wonderful?'

'He can't be,' Carter said, knowing he had to protect the boy. He took a slow step forward, when all he really wanted to do was run from the house, never to return. Papa moved forward, putting himself between Carter and Douglas.

'The boy's mine, Carter.'

'Come with me *now*,' Carter said to Douglas.

'You can't talk to me like that! Tell him, Papa.' Douglas's father walked up to Carter, who was trembling in fear.

'You shouldn't speak to the boy like that. You need to think things over.' Papa placed his hand on Carter's forehead. Something snapped in Carter's mind and he collapsed to the floor. Douglas gasped in horror.

'Papa! What have you done?'

'I'm helping him think things over.'

'What things?' Douglas asked, concerned now.

'Everything.' Douglas's father smiled, absent of any humour. It was as if he'd never seen a smile, but somebody had described what it should look like. The mechanics were correct, but it contained none of the meaning. Douglas edged back towards the stairs, but his father snatched his hand.

53

'Where are you off to? I said I had something to show you.'

'I'm tired,' Douglas mumbled. 'I want to go to bed.'

'Are you disobeying your father?'

'You're not my father.'

'If I'm not your father, then who am I?'

'I don't know.'

Papa opened the front door. A white blanket coated London. Any other time, Douglas would consider it serene and beautiful. Now, it looked unfamiliar and frightening. Papa pulled Douglas out into the frosted air, dragging him along the path. The snow crunched beneath his slippered feet as they walked through the gates that opened and closed of their own accord.

'Where are we going?' Douglas asked through chattering teeth. The thing pretending to be his father gave him that faintly crooked grin.

'Somewhere wonderful.'

Back in the house, Carter screamed and felt he'd never stop.

TWELVE

Elizabeth woke and, for a moment, wondered where she had ended up. Lost in a sea of blankets and pillows, she crawled her way to the surface. The bed linen was the softest she'd ever come across; not scratchy and coarse, and there were no bite marks from tiny creatures sharing her sleeping quarters. She felt as if she was wrapped in warm clouds that extended through the window and across the snowy rooftops. She'd never felt happier and couldn't wait to tell her aunt...

Oh.

Though young, she understood the permanence of death. She was reminded of it on a daily basis as those around her, children and adults, were snatched away by its cold hands. Her parents, her grandparents, younger brother. All gone. But her aunt, the last remnant of her family, vanished forever? Just like that? Leaving Elizabeth all alone? The thought was too huge. She would need to break it down into smaller chunks.

Aunt Julie will never braid my hair again.

Elizabeth was washed away on a tide of grief. She buried her head in the soft pillow and sobbed as she remembered her aunt's delicate fingers bobbing and weaving the strands of Elizabeth's chestnut hair.

When the tears had subsided, she considered the practicalities. She now needed a new home. Perhaps this could be it. The four gentlemen who had taken her in seemed kind enough, if slightly odd. Naturally, she would work hard for them. She knew her place.

A knock on the bedroom door, sharp and efficient. Elizabeth wiped her eyes dry with the sleeve of her nightgown. Tears would now have to be a private matter, shared between only her and the pillow. Who would want a blubbering, snotty mess hanging around and bringing everyone down?

Mrs Burgess poked her head round the door. She was nice, Elizabeth thought, and was in charge no matter what her four employers might say. Elizabeth would need to have her on her side if she was to be able to call this house home.

'Good morning, my lovely. Did you sleep well?' Elizabeth forced a smile and nodded politely. 'Cat still got your tongue?' She nodded again. If she were to speak, she was sure the emotional house of cards she had constructed would come crashing down.

'I'm just about to serve breakfast, if you'd like some. There are clothes in your wardrobe. Come down when you're ready.' Mrs Burgess closed the doors behind her.

Another stream of tears bubbled up. At moments like this, Elizabeth needed to focus her attention on something else; a trick she'd taught herself. She concentrated on the wardrobe until something clicked in her mind. With no hand touching them, the doors gently swung open. A twist of thought and a pale dress floated out from where it hung. Elizabeth tried a few exploratory swoops and then let it pitch and plummet around the room, the delicate fabric flapping like birds' wings. Finally, she guided the dress to its landing on the bed covers and allowed herself a small smile.

Mrs Burgess showed Elizabeth into the breakfast room. Her four hosts were already sitting at a round table. The skinny one was devouring the largest full English breakfast Elizabeth had ever seen with almost heroic ferocity. The funny, angry red-headed man was picking rice from his beard. The hooded man who had brought her to the house silently stirred a cup of tea whilst the handsome fellow was reading the Times newspaper. Mrs Burgess cleared her throat for attention.

'Good morning, gentlemen.'

The handsome man folded the newspaper and placed it on the table. 'Good morning, Elizabeth.' Pointing to an empty chair on the right, he said, 'Please join us. Is there any tea left in the pot, Mrs Burgess?'

Seeing an opportunity to impress, Elizabeth scurried around the table to the ornate silver teapot. The handsome man waved her away. 'You are our guest, young lady. Now, take a seat.' Disappointed, Elizabeth sat down as instructed.

'What would you like to eat?' he asked. 'Porridge? I understand children enjoy it with a spoonful of honey.' Elizabeth shrugged.

'Have you tried kedgeree?' Elizabeth shook her head. 'It's fish, boiled rice, parsley, hard-boiled eggs, curry powder and sultanas.' Elizabeth grimaced. 'You make a good point. It sounds bloody horrendous.'

'Don't use language like that in front of children, Mr Conquest,' Mrs Burgess scolded.

'I apologise.' Conquest pointed to the plate in front of the thin man. 'Would you like what he's eating?' Sausages, eggs, grilled tomatoes, mushrooms, bacon - all piled up like a greasy hillock. Elizabeth couldn't remember the last time she'd eaten bacon. Her eyes grew wide, her mouth watered, and she licked her lips.

'I'll take that as a yes, then.' Conquest turned to Mrs Burgess. 'Mrs Burgess, one of your excellent fry-ups please.' Mrs Burgess smiled at Elizabeth.

'Of course. Would that be with toast and lashing of butter?'

Conquest looked down at Elizabeth with those hypnotic grey eyes, a hint of a smile playing at the corner of his mouth. 'I think it would be rather rude not to. Don't you, Elizabeth?'

'Agreed,' said Mrs Burgess, and she slipped out of the room.

'Would you like a cup of tea?' the thin man asked. Elizabeth nodded. He poured the hot drink into the fine bone china cup placed in front of her. She was in awe. Nobody, especially a man of his status, had ever served her in this manner. 'Help yourself to milk and sugar,' he said with a smile. Elizabeth did.

'Did you sleep well?' Conquest asked.

Elizabeth nodded, slurping her tea.

'Good. If you felt your ears burning, it was because we were talking about you.' She clutched at her ears, an act that made Conquest chuckle kindly. 'A figure of speech. It seems you're a special little girl.' Elizabeth's cheeks flushed red with pride. She tried to hide her grin behind the cup. A girl might get used to this. Conquest leaned forward conspiratorially. 'Do you want to know a secret?'

Elizabeth loved secrets, as long as they weren't her own. She nodded. 'We're a bit special too.' Conquest nodded at the hooded man. 'He doesn't let anybody see him, but you were able to. Perhaps we should formally introduce ourselves. Have you read the bible?'

Elizabeth shifted back in her chair and hoped they weren't like the do-gooder Christians who came into the slums with empty words and futile gestures.

'Don't worry if you haven't. We only turn up at the end. My name's Conquest. This is War, Famine and Death.'

Death waved in what Elizabeth assumed was a jolly manner, Famine smiled politely and War just grunted.

'People call us the Four Horsemen of the Apocalypse, but please don't judge us by our titles. You might have heard of us?' Conquest continued. Elizabeth had heard of them. The Four Horsemen of the Apocalypse summoned the end of the world. Yet, she wasn't sure these men could last five minutes in the pub at the end of her road. 'Maybe we should try to figure out what makes you so special?'

Mrs Burgess entered the room again. 'Excuse me, but there's a gentleman here to see you. Says it's urgent.'

'Send him in,' Conquest replied.

Mrs Burgess coaxed a nervous young man into the breakfast room. Elizabeth could tell from his starched clothing that he was a bureaucrat by trade. He smoothed a cowlick hanging across his forehead.

'I beg your pardon, gentlemen.'

'What is it?' War asked impatiently.

'You are summoned to Downing Street. The Prime Minister has requested it.'

Conquest sighed with irritation. 'What does he want now?'

'I'm not privy to that information, sir.'

This was impressive. Elizabeth wasn't entirely sure who the Prime Minister was, or what he did, but understood it was a very important job. Almost as important as the Queen-Gawd-Bless-Her.

'Very well,' Conquest said. 'We'll be with you momentarily...?'

'Johnson, sir. Right you are, sir,' said the messenger as he backed out of the room.

'Are you coming?' Conquest asked Death.

Death glanced over at Elizabeth almost guiltily. 'Err. No, I have business to attend to.'

Elizabeth didn't think he had anything to feel guilty for. She considered his position with the simple logic of a child. He didn't kill her aunt, or her parents; they'd been sick for some time. He collected them, like Johnson had come for the horsemen just now. He organised things. You needed order. You couldn't have ghosts cluttering up the place.

The other three stood.

'Not you,' Conquest said to War.

'Why not?'

'He doesn't want to see you again. Do I have to remind you what happened last time?'

'I didn't know it was his cat. It was an accident,' War said gruffly.

'You can entertain our guest in our absence.'

'Why can't Mrs Burgess?'

'Some of us have work to do,' she replied sharply. 'I had plans.'

'Like what?' Famine asked.

'Those battle-axes aren't going to organise themselves, y'know.'

'I doubt we'll be too long. You can get a Christmas tree.' Conquest turned to Elizabeth. 'We rarely decorate the house during the festive season, but perhaps we can make an exception for you.' Elizabeth had never decorated a Christmas tree before. Her heart fluttered with excitement at the prospect.

'Now, if you'll excuse us, we must away to Downing Street.' As he stood up, Conquest leaned over and whispered in Elizabeth's ear, 'You seem sensible. Make sure he doesn't get into any trouble.' He winked and Elizabeth couldn't help a giggle.

Death, Famine and Conquest bowed sharply to the ladies.

'We can't keep the Prime Minister waiting,' said Conquest.

'I'll get your breakfast,' Mrs Burgess said to Elizabeth, following the others out of the room.

War and Elizabeth were left alone. They stared at each other suspiciously.

Finally, War said, 'Do you know you're very tiny?'

THIRTEEN

We are not alone in this universe. In fact, the universe itself is not alone. There are an infinite number of alternate realities. Worlds piled upon worlds in a vast complex of possibilities. Parallel universes. Linear universes. Mirror universes. Shadow universes. And darkest timelines where everyone has a goatee and nobody has ever eaten a chocolate Hobnob.

There are dimensions where the Nazis won the Second World War. Dimensions where the dinosaurs survived. There's one dimension where the dinosaurs defeated the Nazis in the Second World War. That's a pretty awesome dimension.

To be honest, it's a right old mess. The fabric between these realities is thinner than you realise; things slip between the gaps all the time. There's a plane of existence where all missing odd socks end up. That universe's inhabitants believe them to be some cryptic message from their gods. Those that maintain the white sports socks are the true word of their Creator wage war against those convinced that knee-length plaid ones are the gospel.

It goes the other way, too. Many of us wonder how we ended up with so many teaspoons. They arrive, unnoticed, through a portal from another Earth where everybody resorts to stirring their tea with a knife. This is how, while Elizabeth ate her breakfast, the creature slipped beneath the city and returned to the Other Place.

The creature took her true form with a sigh. The human body was so constricting.

Almost all children were the same this time of year. They longed for Father Christmas. True, there was the odd exception like tonight's offering, but generally they were grubby ingrates who wanted nothing but distractions and fancies. Their fantasies had shaped her home; a winter wonderland of snow and pines where *they* became the decorations. She hung the new bauble on a frost-encrusted branch. She was a good hostess and the children so loved Christmas. The creature did what she could to make them feel at home while they stayed, no matter how briefly.

She should sleep now. Soon it would be time to feed again and she would need energy to hunt. She curled up in her nest of ice and snow. The hunger would grow; an insatiable craving paying the price for immortality, an emptiness that would never fill. Those millennia she had spent trapped alone with an unsatisfied appetite gnawing at her insides had been a torture she'd thought would never end.

She dreamed of her youth; a happier time long ago, when the simple creatures that wandered the Land Beneath the Skies worshipped her. She didn't remember how she'd found a way into this world from the Other Place. She was smart enough to take advantage of all the delicacies this world offered though. She found she could appear in the form of humans' greatest desires. A simple, yet effective trick. They brought her offerings; their young, in the hope she would deliver what she promised. She never did.

Not all the sacrifices sated her hunger. Only a special few were appetising; those who possessed a psychic talent she could drain. Children were the best; ripe and fresh. The older they were, the more power had leaked out of them making them dry and tasteless.

She went by many names, but her favourite was Esuries. She didn't know what it meant, but enjoyed the simple poetry of the word. As the centuries wore on, Esuries noticed the number of gods and idols had diminished until only a handful remained. Soon after, one or two of the more popular ones set up a monopoly on faith. The devout turned on her, eager to please their new masters like simple-minded pets, burying her beneath the earth. Without sacrifices, she grew weaker. The last of the bright souls she had brought back to feast upon had now turned into dull husks.

Esuries slept and waited. Tawdry, limiting concepts such as time didn't exist in the Other Place. A handful still worshipped her, still spoke her many names. She could sense the faint praise and it kept her alive whilst laying in the cold beneath the living world. She was remembered, which is all any creature wanted to be.

A city grew above her. Upwards, outwards and, eventually, downwards. Then one day: Reawakening. Rebirth. Rejoice. The ground above parted and fell away. She pushed to the surface, through the dark and waste of the world above. Humanity had found their way back to her. They may have moved on and developed new technologies that would've seemed like magic to the earlier faithful, but they still wanted to believe.

Soon, they all would.

FOURTEEN

The cab raced across London with little consideration for other road users. For whatever reason Conquest and Famine had been summoned, it was urgent and time sensitive. They arrived at 10 Downing Street in what Conquest thought must have been some kind of record time. Johnson showed the two available Horsemen of the Apocalypse to the Prime Minister's private study at the back of the building.

Benjamin Disraeli sat behind a dark mahogany desk and stared out the window, down into the small garden below. He tugged at the beard hanging from his chin, deep in thought.

'Your guests are here, Prime Minister,' Johnson announced.

Disraeli turned from the wintry view and smiled politely. 'Gentlemen. How good to see you. Please, have a seat.' He waved at two leather chairs in front of the desk. They sat.

'Can Johnson get you anything?'

'No thank you,' said Conquest.

'Cake,' said Famine, 'and none of this carrot cake nonsense.'

Johnson smiled. 'I'll see what we have in the kitchen.'

'Can you send Inspector Graves in on your way out, please?' Disraeli asked.

'Of course, Prime Minister.' He left the three men alone.

'I note Mr Warfield is conspicuous by his absence,' Disraeli said coolly.

'He sends his apologies,' replied Conquest.

Disraeli pursed his lips. 'I'm sure he does.'

'May I enquire into the health of Mrs Fluffykins?'

'She now walks with a limp and is traumatised whenever she sees a bowl of trifle.'

Famine smiled. 'Still, it was a lovely reception until then.' Conquest glared at Famine before turning back to the Prime Minister.

'Can I ask why you've summoned us?'

Disraeli leant on the desk, his hands clasped together. 'There's been a rather unusual incident involving the family of a close friend of mine. I'm hoping you might get to the bottom of it with your usual discretion.'

A knock on the office door. Disraeli barked, 'Come in.' The door opened and a man with an ill-fitting suit and luxurious moustache entered. 'Ah, Inspector Graves. Thank you for joining us. These are the gentlemen I was telling you about.' Disraeli pointed at Conquest. 'Mr Conway.' Then to Famine. 'Mr Hungerford.'

Inspector Graves shook their hands. 'A pleasure to meet you both,' he said in a thick London accent. 'I've heard many stories.'

In the corridors of Whitehall, the Four Horsemen were known as the Gentlemen of Dubious

Activities. Whenever inexplicable phenomena occurred throughout the Empire, or if some dark operation was to be carried out on behalf of the British government, the Prime Minister of the time knew he could depend on the mysterious residents of 84 McHoan Gardens.

They'd started off as witch-finders, but a reluctance to prosecute the young women coupled with Famine's allergy to cats meant that they were soon relieved of their duties and replaced with someone more eager to get busy with the firelighters.

They'd been surprisingly successful as spies working behind enemy lines during the Napoleonic Wars, even though War's grasp of the French language only extended as far as being able to order cheese. They'd returned with a large amount of classified information and an even greater supply of rather excellent Brie.

Just two years before, they were sent to the Azores to investigate the mysterious disappearance of the crew of the Mary Celeste. They had failed to come up with any concrete conclusions, but had all agreed that it had been an excellent holiday.

'How can we be of help?' Conquest asked.

Graves placed a sepia photograph on the desk. The subject of the portrait was a serious-looking child on a rocking horse.

'This is Douglas Fairchild. We have four independent witnesses who claim to have seen his father take him from his home in the middle of last night.'

Conquest slid the photograph back towards Graves. 'We don't involve ourselves with domestic matters.'

Graves and Disraeli exchanged a nervous glance. 'His father died three years ago.'

Conquest considered this for a moment. 'Well, that sounds like something that would interest us,' he said, passing the photograph to Famine.

Johnson entered the office carrying a plate. 'I'm very sorry,' he said. 'All we have are scones.'

Famine beckoned him over. 'That will be fine.'

Johnson placed the plate on the desk. 'If there's nothing else, I'll get back to work.'

'That will be all, thank you, Johnson,' Disraeli said with a smile. When Johnson had left, the conversation resumed.

'His mother is sick with worry,' Disraeli said.

'Obviously,' Famine said between bites of scone.

'Our usual lines of inquiry have proved fruitless,' Graves said. 'When the Prime Minister was made aware, he suggested that you might be able to help.'

'And what is your involvement in this, sir?' Conquest asked the Prime Minister.

'Arthur Fairchild was a dear friend. Before he died, I made a promise to keep his family safe. All the resources of my government are at your disposal. Find him. Please.'

'We can try. I assume he was taken from his bedroom?'

'Yes, sir. The butler tried to stop them leaving the house.'

'Then I think our first priority is to go to the scene of the crime and talk to him.'

'Of course,' Graves replied. 'Though I feel I should warn you he's been...' He searched for the right words... 'affected by what he experienced.'

'I understand. Let's go,' Conquest said.

'I'm still eating,' Famine protested. Conquest sighed with exasperation.

'Fine. You can bring them with you, just don't get crumbs in the carriage.'

FIFTEEN

The snow stopped falling, the clouds drifting away to reveal a blue sky so crisp that War felt he could shatter it with a well-aimed snowball. He'd lasted a long time before deciding to take Elizabeth out of the house. In the Victorian age, polite society deemed that children should be seen and not heard. War was of the belief they should be neither, just to be on the safe side.

As far as he was concerned, they started off as chubby, helpless lumps and then became so much worse as their wordless screams were replaced by opinions; almost all of them wrong. They simply weren't of any use to him. They were too small to carry a broadsword, too light to put in a cannon and you couldn't even shove them up a chimney any more, thanks to Lord Shaftesbury.

As he trudged his way along the snow-carpeted streets, Elizabeth scampered around him like a small excitable puppy. He wondered how he had fallen so far; from commanding mighty armies to babysitting. The girl seemed thrilled with the whole plan to get a Christmas tree. It seemed ridiculous to him to cut down a mighty evergreen in its prime, drag and squeeze it into a tiny house and then throw it out by Twelfth Night. Christmas trees belonged to the long list of human activities, along with tea and ballet, that baffled War. Actually, theatre in general had bothered him since he'd known William Shakespeare briefly in the 1620s. The relationship turned sour when Will rejected his suggestion to end Romeo and Juliet with a song and dance number.

He and Elizabeth stopped to annihilate a group of street urchins in a snowball fight. War was impressed with Elizabeth's ruthlessness in battle. She showed no mercy, even when the smallest ragamuffin begged her not to shove a ball of ice down his shirt. Ivan the Terrible himself would've hesitated upon hearing those screams.

Leaving a trail of the vanquished behind, they continued on until War felt an urgent tug on his sleeve. He looked down to see Elizabeth pulling him towards a narrow alley. A group of ne'er-do-wells huddled over a game of Find the Lady.

The dealer was a shabby individual, paper-thin skin stretched over a bird-like skull with more eyes than teeth. Wrapped in beaten leathers, he placed three playing cards onto a wooden box in front of him: two black kings and a queen of hearts.

'Lay-dees and gennelmen,' he barked. 'Step right up. The Queen of Hearts is the winning card. Watch it closely. If you point it out the first time, you win.' In one fluid motion, he turned the cards over and shuffled them, his fingers skipping over the bent and dog-eared cards as he threw them across the box lid.

'Follow it with your eyes as I shuffle. Here it is, and now here, now here and now where?' He looked up at the crowd. 'Who will go me a shilling?' He stabbed a finger at an onlooker, 'For a shilling, sir. Can you find the lady? If your sight is quick enough, you beat me and I pay. If not, I take your money. It's a plain and simple game, but you can't always tell.'

The onlooker placed a shilling in front of the middle card. The dealer flipped it over to reveal one of the Kings. He then flipped the other two cards over to reveal the Queen was the one on the left. He pocketed the money.

'Hard luck, sir, but my name is Crafty Larry, and this is my regular trade, to move my hands quicker than your eyes.' He turned the cards over and moved them around again. 'Who will be next? Cherchez la femme, lads. Cherchez la femme.'

Elizabeth tried to drag War over to the crowd, but he wouldn't budge. 'No, he's a con artist. It's a card trick. He'd just take any money you had.' She dropped his sleeve and skipped over to the game, anyway. 'When I say no, I mean no,' War called after her. 'It's not a starting off point to begin negotiations.' Elizabeth had already barged her way through the crowd, slipping between the players' legs until she reached the front. Crafty Larry looked up.

'I take no bets from paupers, cripples or children.' War shoved the crowd aside and stood behind Elizabeth. Crafty Larry took in War's expensive clothing. A small smile tugged at the corner of his mouth. He'd reeled in a big fish. 'Or maybe your father fancies a flutter? What about it, sir? Fancy trying your luck?'

War harrumphed. 'Perhaps we can use this opportunity as a life lesson.'

Crafty Larry showed them where the Queen of Hearts was and shuffled the three cards. Soon the cards came to a rest. 'Where is she, l'il lady?'

War handed Elizabeth a coin. Without hesitation, she placed it in front of the left card. War rolled his eyes. It was obviously the middle card. Crafty Larry looked nervously at Elizabeth, the coin and the card. He turned the card over. The Queen of Hearts. 'That's correct, young lady. Well done.'

Elizabeth took her winnings and placed them back down on the upturned box.

'I think you've played enough,' Crafty Larry said.

War took a step forward. 'If the girl wants another go, then you'll give her another go.'

Crafty Larry swallowed hard. 'Of course, sir.' He shuffled the cards, concentrating as hard as he could, palming the cards as much as he dared while keeping his trickery unnoticed.

Elizabeth found the lady. And she did for the next nineteen games. No matter what sleight of hand Crafty Larry tried, however he might try to distract or misdirect the little cow, she always knew where the card was. What she was doing was impossible, and she was taking him to the cleaners. He didn't dare say anything, as even though her old man looked like a ponce in his finery, he was built like a brick shithouse. Her streak was broken only by the arrival of a police officer.

'Rozzers! Scarper!' yelled a lookout. A flurry of activity and, in a moment, War and Elizabeth were standing in a deserted alleyway.

'Everything all right here?' the policeman asked War.

'Yes, officer.'

The policeman tipped his helmet. 'I'd suggest you and your daughter don't loiter here. There are some unpleasant characters around.'

'Thank you, officer. We were just leaving.'

When the policeman had rounded the corner, War handed to Elizabeth the coins he'd taken from the dealer. She stared at the stack in her hand; she'd never seen so much money before. War stared at her just as hard - she was a curiosity to be puzzled over and figured out.

'Let's get that tree,' he said.

SIXTEEN

The two constables outside the wrought iron gates of the Fairchild home stood to attention as Graves marched past, Conquest and Famine following in his wake. He strode up the path with purpose, bursting through the front door and startling the young policeman loitering in the cavernous hallway.

Behind Graves, Conquest cast a keen eye over the expensive furniture and ornaments. The property was almost as grand as the Four Horsemen's own. It would be a lovely place to live if it wasn't for the hysterical sobbing coming from the drawing room. Graves pointed to a spot on the deep rug.

'The parlour maid found the butler there, curled up and screaming bloody murder.'

'He's only just calmed down, but he's still not right,' the policeman said. 'Sir,' he added, remembering himself.

Graves nodded. A no-nonsense attitude. He understood the gravity of the situation and the need to bring the case to a swift conclusion. 'Thank you, constable.'

'The boy's room is up here?' Conquest asked, pointing up the stairs.

'Yes, sir. Second door on the left.'

The three investigators climbed the stairs to the bedroom, leaving the constable in the hall. Forensic science being in its infancy, two burly policemen were stomping around the room in dirty work boots, turning over possessions, destroying evidence, as they looked for any clues.

'What have we got here, Sarge?' asked Graves.

The larger of the two policemen wiped his hands on his uniform. 'Well, guv, the nanny put the boy to bed at round eight o'clock last evening. He was next seen leaving the property at approximately three o'clock this morning with a gentleman fitting the description of his late father. There is no evidence of forced entry.'

Conquest walked over to the bed and turned the crumpled sheets. With nothing of interest there, he dropped to his knees and looked under the ornate wooden bed frame. A glimmer in the shadows caught his eye. He reached under the bed and his hand grasped something small and round.

'I'd like the officers to leave now,' he said, getting to his feet. The policemen looked to Graves for confirmation. Graves nodded in agreement.

'Get yourself a cup of tea, lads.' They left without a word, closing the door behind them. The room was still, toys scattered on the floor, a crumpled bed. It was if Douglas had woken up, seen the snow and run outside to play.

Conquest opened his hand and presented a small Christmas bauble to the others; red, green and exquisitely patterned with silver. He gripped the string between a thumb and finger and let it spin and dance as he considered the intricate designs.

'What do you think of this?' he asked, throwing the tiny globe to Famine. Famine caught it with one hand and examined it. He sniffed and then tasted it with the tip of his tongue. Scrunching his nose up in disgust, he held it out at arm's length.

'This thing is dripping with magic.'

Conquest turned to Graves. 'I think we'd like to talk to the butler now.'

Carter was in the kitchen, wrapped in a blanket and rocking back and forth on a wooden chair. Famine and Conquest trod lightly on the stone floor, approaching him as they would a startled animal.

'Mr Carter?' Conquest asked. Carter looked up, fearful eyes darting left and right. His gaze settled on the men standing in front of him. Noticing their fine clothes, he tried and failed to pull together the remaining strands of his dignity.

'Yes, sir?'

'We're friends of the Fairchilds. Here, take a sip of this.' Conquest passed Carter a glass of whisky. Carter tried to bring it to his lips, but his trembling hands caused the liquid to spill. Conquest wrapped his fingers around Carter's and gently lifted the glass to his mouth.

Conquest waited as the alcohol warmed and relaxed Carter. Only when his shaking had subsided did Conquest ask, 'Would you care to tell us what you saw last night?'

The shivering returned, Carter's limbs spasming and trembling. He spoke slowly and deliberately, dragging each word up to his mouth. 'As I told the constable, Mr Fairchild and Master Douglas were leaving the house. I tried to stop them.' He grabbed Conquest's arm and stared deeply into his eyes. 'He showed me things. Such terrible things. I can still see them.' Carter released Conquest from his grip and scratched his head violently, grey hair thrown in every direction. 'The bees! The bees are in my head! I can feel them crawling and buzzing in there!'

Conquest and Famine took several attempts to each grab an arm and hold them down. They whispered soothing words until Carter relaxed and his ragged breathing returned to normal. His head dropped, and he stared at the grey floor. 'I saw its true form,' he said in a cracked voice, 'It was pure evil.' Conquest shared a glance with Famine, then reached into his pocket and took the bauble out.

'Do you recognise this?' Carter raised his head. When he saw the globe, he threw himself backwards. The chair clattered on the hard stone as Carter dragged himself along, trying to put as much distance as possible between him and the innocent-looking Christmas decoration. Rolling onto his side, he balled himself up into a foetal position and, muttering, rocked from side to side. Conquest strained to hear what Carter was saying.

'They're hanging in my head. The baubles are dangling behind my eyes. They'll never stop swinging. Help me.' Graves entered the room and gasped.

'Have you broken my witness?'

Conquest sighed. 'Poor fellow. He'll be fine in a few days. Just keep him away from any Christmas trees.' He pocketed the bauble to spare Carter further agony and looked to Famine. 'Who do we know enjoys tormenting the innocent and has an evil form?'

SEVENTEEN

Beelzebub sat in his cramped office in a quiet back street in Soho, staring across the scratched and stained desk at what could only be described as a small man-shaped collection of dirt and unfortunate skin conditions.

'I'm sorry? You want to do what?' He glanced at the piece of paper in front of him, 'Mr Miller?'

Miller cleared his throat, thick phlegm rattling around his chest like gravel in a can, and repeated, 'I'd like to sell my soul.' Beelzebub tugged at a loose thread on his faded jacket.

'And what makes you think I'm in the market for that sort of thing, Mr Miller?'

Miller screwed his face up in puzzlement. 'You're the Devil, Satan, Beelzebub. I believe the transaction is that I pledge you my eternal soul in exchange for my heart's desire.'

'What? And then you're doomed to the eternal damnation of Hell? That sort of thing?'

Miller brightened now that Beelzebub was on the same wavelength. 'That sort of thing, yes.'

'And why would I want to do that?' asked Beelzebub. 'What do I get out of it?'

'Another soul for your Legion of the Damned.'

'And what would I do with a legion, damned or otherwise?' Beelzebub replied testily. He leaned forward, his hands clasped, and rested his elbows on the desk. 'I will teach you something, Mr Miller. The universe does not care about you. It doesn't care about anyone. It is apathetic to the concepts of good and evil. There is no Heaven and Hell, no punishment or reward. There is only an interminable forever. The Almighty, whoever he may be, has grown weary of you. Like a petulant schoolboy bored with the ant farm he demanded, he has thrown you aside and moved onto his next five-minute wonder. You are alone in this Godforsaken world. We all are.'

'But you have dominion over all the Underworld.'

Beelzebub sighed. 'Do you know what I have dominion over? A small flat in Islington. If you can find any lakes of fire there, you're more than welcome to throw yourself in.'

Miller looked crushed. 'What do I do now? I was kind of pinning my hopes on you.'

'Well, you shouldn't have done that. Remember who you're dealing with. I'll give you some advice. Find yourself a nice girl, or a nice boy, and do whatever you want. Whether you live a blameless life or drown yourself in sin, time will simply pass its bored gaze over your existence and you will be forgotten by all those who follow. You can show yourself out.'

Miller grabbed his hat, muttered a goodbye and left.

Beelzebub tried to get on with some work, but his mind wouldn't settle. He missed the good old days when his time was filled with devilry. It was easy to push and provoke these meat puppets at the dawn of the age of man. They were full of exciting new emotions and interesting new bodily fluids, easy to manipulate into all sorts of compromising positions. The Roman Empire was a blast. Now there was a group of guys and gals who were into Having a Good Time and if someone got eaten by a tiger in the process then all the better.

Beelzebub was particularly proud of the Spanish Inquisition. Not only did he persuade a group of men to act out their deepest and darkest of desires but he actually convinced them they were doing it in the name of God. Pointy things shoved in and out of orifices were apparently the Lord's teachings. He'd laughed for a week over that one.

The Victorian Age, however, was too much like hard work. Everyone was so prim and proper, they were all so bloody repressed. He really had to put the effort in to get some temptation going.

There was a knock at the door.

'Come in,' Beelzebub commanded. Colin, Beelzebub's minion, entered carrying a cup of tea.

'I thought you might like a cuppa, Master.'

'Thank you, Colin.'

Colin shuffled across the office, dragging his left leg behind him. With his grotesque features, humped back and limp, the only career available to him was as a henchman to an evil and/or mad scientist. The job market had dried up recently and when Beelzebub found him on the side of a road in Whitechapel holding a sign reading 'WILL ASSIST IN THE REANIMATION OF CORPSES FOR FOOD', Colin made the sideways move into minionry.

Colin placed the cup on the edge of the desk and lurked; another skill he'd listed on his CV.

'Is there anything else, Colin?' Beelzebub asked, irritated by his presence.

'With all due respect, sir, you don't seem your normal wrathful self.'

Beelzebub leaned back in his chair. 'Oh, Colin, I should gouge your eyes out with a wooden spoon for such impertinence.'

'Again, sir?'

'But, for once, you are correct. I'm filled with a sense of...' Beelzebub searched for the right word to express his mood.

'Ennui, sir?'

'Yes, you've put your finger on it. Superb. In fact, you can have one of your fingers back.' Beelzebub opened a drawer and tossed a severed finger to Colin, who failed to catch it, and it bounced sadly on the floor.

'Thank you, sir,' Colin said as he bent awkwardly to pick his digit up.

Through the frost-encrusted window, Beelzebub gazed down on the multitude of humans filling the street below. 'They used to worship me, Colin. They would gather in masses and sacrifice themselves for me. I grew strong on the blood spilled in my name. Now I'm lucky if a chicken is beheaded as a tribute.'

Colin looked up from the delicate process of reattaching his finger. 'I could pop out and get one if you'd like? Could sacrifice it during my lunch break? They have some for sale down the market.' Beelzebub patted Colin on the arm, making him stitch his hand to his jacket.

'Bless you, my freakishly deformed minion, but please don't.'

'Oh, I almost forgot. There's a gentleman here to see you. He declined to give me his name.'

'What does he want?'

'He wouldn't say.'

'Well, what does he look like?' Beelzebub asked with growing impatience. Colin shrugged.

'Well dressed, good looking...'

Beelzebub groaned.

'Come in, Conquest,' he shouted. Conquest entered the room, his face stern. This wasn't a social call.

'Beezelbub,' Conquest said with a nod. Beelzebub rolled his eyes.

'How are you?'

'I'm fine, thank you.'

'And the other three?'

'I don't have time for small talk.'

'Well, you never write. You never visit.'

'Cup of tea, sir?' Colin asked.

'No, thank you. I won't be staying long,' Conquest replied.

'Actually, where are the other three?' Beelzebub peered out of the doorway. 'It's unusual to see one of you on your own.'

'War and Death are busy. Famine is downstairs thinking about what he's done.'

'Crumbs in the carriage again?' Beelzebub asked.

'You wouldn't think it would be so difficult,' Conquest replied, the frustration in his voice palpable.

'Why are you here?'

Conquest was glad he was able get to the point. He didn't want to spend any more time in this creature's company than he had to. He pulled the bauble from his pocket and passed it to Beelzebub.

'Does this have anything to do with you?'

Beelzebub studied the sphere with wonder. 'It's beautiful,' he gasped, 'but I've never seen it before.'

Conquest folded his arms. 'And I'm supposed to take the word of the King of Lies?'

Beelzebub looked baffled. 'Then why did you come here? It's lucky you're pretty because you're not too smart.'

'You had nothing to do with this?'

Beelzebub threw his arms wide. 'Look what I've become. Reduced to this state. Industry and science are the new masters. We're myths, cautionary tales humanity tells its children.' He held the bauble out to Conquest. 'You can feel the power in this. Whoever created this is idolised, is worshipped, is dangerous. There are other monsters in this world and beyond. You know that. Why don't you try annoying one of them for a change?'

Conquest looked doubtful. 'I wouldn't know where to start.' Beelzebub handed the bauble back.

'What about that friend of yours? Christou? He's been known to enjoy a cult or two. Perhaps he knows about this.'

'Why are you being so helpful?' Conquest asked, his eyes narrowing. 'I normally have to beat this sort of thing out of you.'

'Do you really have to ask? Whoever that thing belongs to will only get stronger until it reigns over the world, and there's only one person who's going to do that. Me.'

EIGHTEEN

To War's surprise, it had been a thoroughly pleasant day once it got going. Elizabeth hadn't spoken, but seemed more relaxed in his company. They left the alleyway and went for mulled wine and hot chocolate in a nearby coffee shop, which Elizabeth had insisted on paying for with the winnings. War watched her eat the thickly-whipped cream with a spoon. The smile on her chocolate-smeared lips showed she'd never tasted such decadence.

'How did you do that?' he asked. Elizabeth gave him a quizzical look from behind a mountain of foam. 'With the cards,' he explained. 'I've never seen anyone do that before.' She shrugged, her primary form of communication. 'Could you see him palming the cards? Did he have a tell?'

She thought about the question for a moment, then tapped the side of her forehead with her index finger and, with the same finger, tapped the table.

'You knew where the card was?' War asked, sensing he was on the verge of a breakthrough. 'A sort of sixth sense?' But Elizabeth was concentrating on the drink in front of her, carving the cream into shapes with the back of the spoon. War drank his wine in silence.

They chose a tree and, after War's protests were ignored, took the new underground train back to McHoan Gardens. It'd been a long time since War had had a new experience, and as they travelled through the subterranean tunnels, her wonder at everything was rubbing off on him. He was beginning to see how humans got so attached to the young.

The tree arrived at the house, and they discovered it was slightly too tall for the library, causing the top branch to bend against the ceiling. War brought dust-covered boxes full of decorations down from a forgotten part of the attic and the two spent the afternoon dressing it.

What they lacked in design talent, they more than made up for in enthusiasm. Soon, it looked like a unicorn had thrown up all over the tree as it creaked under the weight of the glitter and tinsel.

'What would you like Father Christmas to bring you this year?' War asked, looking for a Wise Man for the nativity scene. Elizabeth shrugged. War ploughed on regardless. 'There must be something. I should tell you Father Christmas and I go way back. Of course, back then he was just plain old Jeff Christmas.' Elizabeth smiled.

A pony. The two words appeared in War's head unbidden, as if someone else's thoughts were mixed up with his own. The phrase had a sing-song quality. War crouched down so he was eye level with Elizabeth.

'Did you..?'

Yes.

He scratched the itch at the back of his head. 'Do it again.'

No. He clapped his hands together and laughed. A breakthrough. He didn't care how odd it was. He straightened back up to his full height.

'A pony, you say? I used to have one, you know? A fine steed who served me well in many a battle. Her name was Lemon Drop. She cost me a fortune in sugar lumps, but I miss her.' He glanced down at Elizabeth. Silence. He didn't mind. Small steps. 'I say you can tell a lot about a person's character by how they treat their horse. I reckon you'd treat your horse well.'

War stepped back from the tree to check their work. There was something missing, but War couldn't put his finger on it. Elizabeth went to a box and rummaged until she found a bent and twisted silver star, straightened its arms and held it out to War. He was about to take it from her hand when it floated upwards. Free. Beautiful. Unnatural. Drifting higher, spinning in the late afternoon sun, it nested on a branch just under the ceiling.

War looked from Elizabeth to the star and back again. He didn't know much about children, but he was pretty sure they shouldn't be able to do that. He was in the presence of true magic.

Mrs Burgess poked her head around the library door. 'Are you two playing nicely? Are you friends?'

War and Elizabeth exchanged a glance which told him all he needed to know: that it had been a private moment of shared wonder.

'Yes, Mrs Burgess,' they said together.

NINETEEN

As London grew rapidly and its infrastructure struggled to keep up with the expanding population, it was agreed that the Metropolitan Underground railway was the mass transit solution to take the city into the twentieth century. It was quick, convenient and avoided the fiddly and embarrassing problem of what to do with all the poor people. The first Tube station opened in 1863. They then realised that a second would make the enterprise more useful and, soon, more and more tunnels extended and branched through the clay and rock until it reached the East End.

Conquest, Famine and Graves stood at the edge of one of the building sites. The sun was hanging low in the sky, stretching shadows along the scene in front of them. A deep trench ran parallel to the congested Whitechapel Road as if God himself had scraped his fingernails across the face of the Earth.

Conquest estimated it to be forty feet wide and half as deep, disappearing into a tunnel at the other end, an arch-roofed construction covered in soil. Mounds of earth ran along the top of the trench wall, dusted with snow like a scale model of a mountain range. Below, workmen shored up the sides with wooden planks; a precarious operation where one slip could cause the spoil to slide down and engulf them all. It reminded him of the giant engineering works of ancient times; the great pyramids of Egypt or the aqueducts of Rome. Once again, here was a civilisation working at the limits of their technology and understanding.

The three made their way down a set of rudimentary wooden stairs built into the mud walls. When they reached the bottom, they breathed a sigh of relief before Graves waved his warrant card at the nearest worker.

'Graves of Scotland Yard. Have you seen Archibald Christou?' he barked. The worker pushed his flat cap back and scratched his stubble with a greasy hand.

'The posh fella? Think he might be talking to the foreman,' he replied, pointing over to the tunnel.

They trudged along the trench, the cold mud sucking at their shoes and trouser legs, and Conquest made a mental note to add the cleaning bill to the list of expenses. He spotted Archibald, half-hidden in the darkness of the tunnel entrance, talking to an annoyed-looking man.

'Archibald!' Conquest called out with a wave. Archibald looked around, confused, and smiled when he saw Conquest, beckoning them over. Conquest turned to Graves.

'It might be best if we talk to him alone.'

'Right you are, sir,' replied Graves, who was well aware that whatever was going on here was well above his pay grade. 'I'm sure there are plenty of labour laws being broken around here. That should keep me busy.'

While Graves wandered off to shout at the working classes, Conquest and Famine headed over to Archibald, Famine losing a shoe in the ooze on the way.

'Gentlemen,' Archibald said, shaking their hands.

'How are you?' Conquest asked.

Archibald sighed. 'We're behind schedule. Who would've thought tunnelling beneath the world's largest city would be so difficult? But never mind that. What brings you here?'

Conquest squelched uncomfortably. 'We're investigating a case involving a child who went missing last night.'

'You think I have something to do with it?' Archibald asked, the offence obvious in his tone.

'No, not at all,' Famine replied. 'We wanted your advice as an expert on cults.'

Archibald threw his hands up. 'You try to destroy the Earth just once and nobody lets you forget it.' Conquest fished around in his pocket and produced the bauble. As he handed it over, he noticed a glint in Archibald's eye. Archibald passed it back and forth between both hands as if it was hot. 'It's beautiful,' he whispered.

'Can you tell us anything about it?' Archibald shook his head. Conquest wasn't sure whether it was to answer his question or to clear his mind. He handed the bauble back.

'No, I've seen nothing like it before.' Archibald's manner had grown as cold as the winter air. 'Now, if you'll excuse me, I must get on.'

'Of course. Thank you for your time. I apologise for inconveniencing you.'

'Not at all. You must come by the house for tea soon.'

'That would be delightful. Thank you,' Conquest replied with a smile.

As they turned to leave, Archibald blurted out, 'I hope you find the young boy.'

'So do we,' Conquest said.

'That was a waste of time,' Famine said when they were out of earshot.

'Oh, I don't know,' replied Conquest with a smirk. 'Did you see his reaction when he saw the bauble?'

'No.'

'It was as if he'd seen his heart's desire. He knew what it was. And he said he hoped we found the boy.'

'That was jolly decent of him.'

'I only told him we were looking for a child. Nobody mentioned the gender. I suspect Mr Christou knows more about this case than he's telling us.'

They found Graves yelling at a baffled carpenter whose only crime was using an apprentice as a work bench.

'All done?' he asked as he dropped the workman down into the ooze.

'I'd like someone to tail Mr Christou, Inspector,' Conquest said.

Graves stiffened. 'Is he a suspect?'

'I'm not sure. A witness at the very least.'

'I'll put my best men onto it straight away,' Graves said. 'Where to now?'

Famine checked his pocket watch. 'I make it tea time.'

'Back to the house,' Conquest decided.

'We'd better get going,' Graves said. 'The traffic will be murder at this time.'

Archibald watched Conquest, Famine and the policeman clamber back up the rickety ladder with only 5/6th of the footwear they'd come down with. Once they'd dragged themselves over the ridge and slipped from view, he backed away, further into the tunnel where the sounds of the building site faded until only his boots scuffing on the rocks and soil remained.

'Who were you talking to, darling?' a voice from the shadows asked.

'No-no-nobody,' Archibald stammered into the dark.

'Oh, come now. I thought we said no secrets? What are you hiding?'

Archibald stumbled backwards. 'Nothing.'

A woman stepped into the flickering light of the gas lamps. The fire danced in her radiant green eyes and her auburn hair blew in the breeze that whispered along the rough walls. She had dressed inappropriately for heavy industrial work.

She was in a wedding dress. Though she had been waiting in the cold filth, the silk was spotless. 'I won't ask again. Who were they, my love?'

'St-stop calling me that. You're not her,' he spat. 'You're not Sarah. Sarah's dead.'

The creature that looked like Sarah pressed her body against his and she felt his excitement growing against her unfamiliar curves.

'Oh, but I could be just as good as her,' she whispered in his ear and ran a slender hand across the front of his trousers. She gently squeezed, enjoying the strange pressure against her fingers. 'I'll show you if you tell me.'

'It was some old friends.'

'There's something special about them. Something magical.'

'They're the Four Horsemen of the Apocalypse.' He gulped deeply. 'Well, half of them anyway.'

'I've heard of them. What did they want?'

'Nothing. It was just a social call.'

She squeezed again, this time to cause pain rather than pleasure. 'What. Did. They. Want?'

He gasped. 'They... They were looking for a child. The one you took. They had one of your relics.'

She tilted her head in an approximation of curiosity. 'What did you tell them?'

'Nothing,' Archibald whimpered, 'Nothing at all. I swear.' She gazed into his wet eyes. A moment's consideration.

'I believe you. The Four Horsemen of the Apocalypse and I should be friends, don't you think? Where do they live? I should pay them a visit.'

97

'No. You will not hurt them.'

'Don't worry, my sweet. I just want to talk to them. I want to give them whatever their hearts desire, like I have with you. Tell me, where do they live?' Her hand loosened his belt buckle.

'84 McHoan Gardens.' The words slipped easily from his lips. 'But...' Esuries, the Not-Sarah, placed a finger against Archibald's lips and could feel his warm mammalian breath against her cold skin. It turned her stomach. She pushed him down into the mud with a splat.

'See? That was easy, wasn't it?'

TWENTY

The sun had set by the time Conquest and Famine arrived home. They removed their winter coats in the hallway and, when Conquest opened the cloak-room door, he was surprised to find War curled up beneath a sheepskin jacket.

'What are you doing?' Conquest asked, bemused. War extricated himself from the outerwear, dusted himself down and straightened his waistcoat.

'Playing Hide-and-Seek,' he replied, as if it was the most obvious thing in the world.

'Where's Elizabeth?'

'Well, if I've been successful in throwing her off the scent, somewhere upstairs.'

Conquest hung the coats up on two available hooks. 'I take it you've coped looking after her?'

'Oh, yes. We've had a marvellous time,' War said, beaming, before remembering his reputation. 'I mean, it's been bearable. I've conquered various continents, so I'm more than capable of looking after a small child.'

'Wonderful to hear. Is Death around?'

'He was skulking around the library the last time I saw him.'

'Excellent. Time for a house meeting.' Conquest shut the cloakroom door and herded his friends into the library. 'Oh, and War?'

'Yes?'

'You've got chocolate in your beard.'

The Four Horsemen settled into their favourite chairs in the library. Famine had found snacks and was happily munching away. Opposite, Death was puffing on a pipe. He'd taken up smoking a few years before to look more distinguished, even though War had pointed out you couldn't get more bloody distinguished than swanning around everywhere in a black cloak and cowl and carrying a sodding great scythe.

Conquest recounted the events of the day; the visit to Downing Street, the child's bedroom and the suspicious conversation with Archibald Christou. He showed the photograph of Douglas Fairchild to Death, who confirmed that he hadn't met him in the last twenty-four hours. They then passed the strange bauble around. They all agreed there was something powerful and magic about it, but nobody knew anything more.

Death tapped the bowl of the pipe against the ashtray balanced on the chair's arm. 'Where do we go from here?'

Conquest shrugged. 'I don't have a clue. Any ideas, War?' War sat in silence, arms crossed. If Conquest didn't know any better, he would've said the living embodiment of combat and bloodshed was sulking.

'Is anything wrong, War?' Conquest asked. 'Anything you'd like to share with the group?'

'No, not at all,' War replied, thin-lipped.

'Fair enough.' Conquest turned to Famine.

'It's just that we've been sat here for five minutes and nobody has mentioned the bloody Christmas tree,' War blurted.

He pointed to the tree at the far end of the library, which looked as if it had been caught in a devastating explosion in a department store's Christmas section.

Famine rolled his eyes. 'Well, we have slightly more pressing matters to deal with.'

'Elizabeth and I spent a long time on the decorations.'

Conquest patted War on the hand. 'The tree looks lovely. You've both done an excellent job.'

'Thank you very much. A bit of appreciation, that's all I was looking for.'

Death looked around. 'Where is Elizabeth?'

The door flew open, slamming into the wall. Framed in the doorway, Elizabeth was a pocket-sized vision of wrath and fury. Hands on hips, rage written all over her face. 'You cheated, War.'

War sank back into his seat. 'It's not my fault if you're not trained in counter-espionage and guerrilla battle tactics. What do they teach you at school, these days? You said you could find anything.'

'I was playing fair.' Elizabeth punched War playfully until he picked her up by the scruff of her neck. She lashed out at the air with tiny fists, laughing and squealing.

'Would chocolate make things better?'

Elizabeth nodded furiously. War dropped her onto his knee and pulled a chocolate bar from his beard. He passed it to her, and she devoured it. War looked up and saw three pairs of eyes staring at him. Well, two pairs of eyes. He assumed Death had the same expression as Conquest and Famine.

'Oh,' he said. 'She's talking now. Or, at least she is when not cramming her mouth full of food. Did you know how much they eat?' Elizabeth swallowed the last of the chocolate. When she saw the bauble in Conquest's hand, she slid off War's knee and crossed the floor. She moved slowly, not taking her eyes off the decoration, as if approaching a dangerous and unpredictable animal. When she was sure it wouldn't do anything untoward, she took it and examined it minutely. Conquest watched her with fascination.

'I had a dream about this,' Elizabeth whispered. 'She puts them inside and takes them to the Other Place.'

'Who is she?' asked Conquest.

Elizabeth shrugged. 'She's different every time, but she's a monster.'

Conquest leaned forward. 'And she puts who inside?'

Elizabeth looked up at him. 'Boys and girls. They're the same as me. She feeds off them.'

'She eats them?' Conquest asked with horror. Elizabeth shook her head.

'No, she keeps them prisoner. They have magic. That's what she feeds on.'

'What's the other place?' Conquest was probing gently, not wanting to upset her such that she'd retreat into silence.

'Her home. Somewhere else. Not here.'

'Where?'

'Below the ground.'

'Can you find it?'

She scrunched her face up, mulled the question over. 'No.'

'Can you tell us where she is now?'

Elizabeth stopped and closed her eyes, then opened them wide. A tiny hand reached out and grabbed Conquest's arm. 'She's close.'

A knock on the library door made everybody jump in terror. It was Mrs Burgess, looking troubled and nervous.

'I'm glad you're all here,' she said, her voice wavering. 'I have something to say.' Conquest gathered himself together and managed a smile. He noticed Mrs Burgess was clutching an envelope crumpled by nervous hands.

'Please, come in.' Mrs Burgess entered the room, smiling at Elizabeth, who scurried back over to War's side.

'Gentlemen,' she said, then swallowed hard. She took a deep breath and continued, 'I shall keep this brief. I'd just like to say it has been a wonderful, if sometimes baffling, experience to work for you. Now, though, it is time I move on and so I must give you notice of leaving your service. This letter should explain everything.' She held the envelope out in a shaking hand. Conquest took it gently while the others murmured in shocked protest. He opened it and unfolded the piece of paper contained inside.

'Is it the money? I'm sure we can come to some arrangement,' Famine asked.

'No, sir,' Mrs Burgess replied.

'Is it because of that time when War--?'

'No, I've made my peace with that.' Conquest finished reading and passed the letter to Famine on his left.

'You are to set sail for the Americas?'

'Yes, Sir.'

'When?'

'Christmas Day, but we plan to take the train to Southampton on the Eve.'

'So soon?' Famine asked as he gave the letter to Death. 'That's only two days away.'

'Mr Burgess is keen to start our new life.'

'But why America? It's full of Americans.' War asked.

'Mr Burgess says it's the land of opportunity.'

War sneered. 'I hear the President's a drunk.'

'So are most of our politicians,' said Conquest.

'A fair point,' War conceded.

'Surely there's something we can do to make you stay?' asked Famine.

'I'm sorry, sir, but our passage has already been arranged. It's what we both want. I can recommend several other ladies qualified to replace me.'

Conquest stood and took her hands in his. 'Then you shall go with our blessing, though I doubt you could be replaced. I speak for all of us when I say you came into our home as our employee, but you leave as our friend.'

The other Horsemen murmured in agreement. Mrs Burgess wiped a tear from her eye. 'Thank you, sir, I can't tell you how much that means. Now, if you'll excuse me I need to start your dinners.'

'Nonsense,' Famine said. 'It will be my honour to prepare a feast in your name. Tonight, you shall dine with us.'

'I couldn't...'

'We insist,' Conquest said.

'Too bloody right we do,' agreed War. Mrs Burgess pulled a handkerchief from her pocket and blew her nose with a moist rasp.

'Thank you.'

'Think nothing of it,' Famine said. 'Now, first thing's first. Where is the kitchen?'

'Follow me,' Mrs Burgess said with a smile.

'Bugger,' muttered Death when Mrs Burgess and Famine had left the room.

'Do you mind? There's children present,' War said. Death looked at this new, responsible War with surprise.

'Sorry.'

TWENTY-ONE

Although Archibald had given her the address, Esuries would've found the Four Horsemen's home with ease, anyway. Trails of magic were scattered throughout the city like breadcrumbs and they all led back to the imposing property. She scouted the building, long limbs creeping around well-pruned shrubs and flowerbeds, and found the residents deep in conversation when she peered through a window. The power of those creatures was obvious; an ancient magic at least as old as her own. How had they not come to her attention sooner? She almost fell backwards in shock when she saw what one of them held in his hands. Archibald was right. How had they come by the bauble? She must've left one behind somewhere, an act so foolish it was almost human. Perhaps she'd spent too long imitating them. Does form influence behaviour?

Esuries soon forgot these matters when the little girl appeared, her power flooding Esuries's senses and overwhelming her thoughts. The child shone like a beacon, drawing the creature in. She was what Esuries had waited for all those hungry, interminable centuries living hand to mouth. Her head was still spinning, drunk on the energy the child gave out, when another female entered the room.

Nothing special about this one, though; dull and lifeless as the majority of her species. Esuries slunk beneath the window. She'd never taken so many at once, but would allow herself to be greedy this one time. She would have four now and was already making plans for the youngest. That supernova energy would be a special treat. A life-changing opportunity. And not just for Esuries.

As she moved to the front of the house, she wondered what form she would take. She was often surprised by the vastness of the human imagination and the distance between their place in the world and what they ultimately desired. Giddy and nervous as a child sneaking out for a midnight feast, she took a moment to compose herself. Then, Esuries knocked on the front door.

Famine had removed every item from the kitchen drawers and was loudly complaining there were no ostriches in the larder, ruining his plans for a nineteen-bird roast. Whoever it was calling at the door, Mrs Burgess was grateful for the diversion.

A wicker basket sat on the doorstep. At first Mrs Burgess thought a lazy deliveryman had left it, but was shocked to see a newborn baby swaddled in blankets. She looked around the street for its mother, but couldn't see anything in the thick fog.

She brought the basket into the warmth, shutting the lethal cold outside. It was almost unbelievable; she'd dreamed of a moment like this for years. That a mother, desperate for her child to have a better life, would give them up hoping someone would raise and love them as their own. Her heart ached as the child yawned, its tiny hands grasping at the air, looking for comfort. Whispering words of reassurance, she carried it into the library. War looked up from the book he was reading to Elizabeth. He took a moment to register what was in Mrs Burgess's arms.

'Where the bloody hell did that come from?'

Conquest folded his newspaper. 'Well, when a mummy and daddy love each other very much, they get certain urges...'

'Oh, do be quiet,' War replied testily. 'You know what I mean. Is there a sign hanging above our front door saying, "All Waifs and Strays Taken In Here"?'

'She was sat there on the doorstep. Nobody around. I had to bring her in from the cold.'

'Of course you did, Mrs Burgess,' Conquest said with a reassuring smile.

Mrs Burgess placed the basket on a side table, the baby gurgling happily to herself. She bent down to pick it up, but War jumped to his feet.

'Don't touch it! If it has your scent, the mother will abandon it!'

'I'm pretty sure that's hamsters you're thinking of,' said Death. War sat back down.

'Oh, right. Carry on then.'

A slightly singed Famine burst into the library brandishing a frying pan. Everyone turned and watched the wisps of smoke rising from his hair.

'There's absolutely nothing to worry about,' he said, trying to approximate a relaxed grin, 'but, just out of interest, does anybody know where the fire extinguisher is?' Conquest rolled his eyes.

'I'll show you.' Then, an unfamiliar sensation hit him like a punch to the gut. Confusion and fear.

The baby was writhing in its blankets. Conquest would've said it was having a tantrum, but it made no sound. Then its arms and legs twisted and stretched with a sickening splitting and snapping of bones. The head rolled back, replaced by something with far too many eyes. The abomination grew, crushing the basket beneath its weight, as sinuous limbs sprouted from cold, grey flesh.

War instinctively moved in front of Elizabeth, his hand scrabbling blindly, searching for the sword resting at the side of the chair.

'You have something I want,' the creature said, a voice like shards of glass sliding over each other. Conquest stroked the bauble in his pocket as his nerves desperately regrouped.

'I'm sorry, but we're completely out of mince pies.'

The monster, this affront to nature, pointed a spiny limb over Conquest's shoulder. 'The girl.' The Four Horsemen closed ranks, shielding Elizabeth, who was trying to peer around the wall of bodies.

'I think you should leave, Mrs Burgess,' Conquest said with calm authority. Mrs Burgess, a whimper escaping her lips, backed towards the door. Her senses had already bolted and she quickly followed.

The creature took a step forward on spindly legs and, without warning, lashed out with some kind of tentacle, connecting squarely with the side of

Conquest's face with a wet slap. The force spun him around and he crashed into a shelf, scattering books across the floor.

Famine swung the heavy frying pan, but the monster wrapped an arm around the handle and plucked it from his hand. She smashed it down on the top of Famine's burnt head, making him stagger around drunkenly.

War located his sword and ran towards the mass of arms and tentacles. Swinging wildly, the blade tore a chunk of flesh from the thick trunk of muscle, spraying dark blood across the carpet. The monster screamed and flailed in agony, sending the contents of shelves crashing to the floor like a heavy leather landslide.

Those few seconds of distraction were enough for the Four Horsemen. They used whatever weapons came to hand. Famine reclaimed his frying pan, Conquest plucked a red-hot poker from the fire, and Death picked up a weighty tome on Medieval tax reform. With centuries of military training, they charged the creature; beating, slashing, stabbing and poking until they forced it towards the large bay window. Cornered, with no other way out, the monster threw its weight at the thick glass. The wooden frame splintered, shattering the window and, in one leap, the creature disappeared into the freezing night.

The Horsemen stood in stunned silence, the glass crunching under their slippers. War spun around, his eyes frantically searching the room.

'Elizabeth?' he called, a note of panic in his voice. He sighed with relief as she crawled out from behind an armchair. 'Ah, good stuff. Excellent to see you,' he said with a gruff air.

Death stared through the ragged remains of the window. 'What was that thing?'

'I don't know, but I think we've found the prime suspect in our case,' Conquest said. 'Could you sense it?'

'Yes. The same as when I held the bauble,' Famine said.

'What does it want with Elizabeth?' They turned to look at the girl. Famine gasped, covering his mouth with a hand...

'Oh, bloody hell. I've left the oven on.'

TWENTY-TWO

Keeping to the shadows, Esuries limped through the London streets. She stumbled and blundered between trees, the powdery snow falling from branches onto her hot, wet skin providing relief before she slipped beneath the city to the Other Place.

Curling up in her nest of stone, she nursed the injured limb. She hadn't felt pain for so long it had lost all meaning until tonight. Her body was a canvas of slices, cuts and scratches. She had been foolish again, distracted by the dazzling brilliance of the girl's gifts and underestimating the power of those Horsemen, and had paid the price.

Tonight's events made the hunger worse, the dull ache gnawing away at the pit of her stomach. Like a starving man shown a magnificent feast laid out in front of him, only to have it cruelly snatched away. She took a trinket from the nearest tree and held it close to her body. A tiny morsel. Esuries remembered this child. He wanted a puppy, one of the few creatures in that world above more pathetic than the humans; always so desperate to please. Trained and subservient. Sickening.

Stronger after her snack, Esuries considered her next move. If the opportunity arose to take the other four she would do it, but there would be no wavering from her goal this time. With so much power in that tiny, flimsy body, she wanted Elizabeth more than anything, convinced the girl was what she'd waited an eternity for. If Esuries possessed that energy, she could do anything. No longer would she have to hide beneath the ground amongst the filth and vermin. She could make humanity forget about their absent gods and take her place on the throne of the world.

But she couldn't do this alone. Help was needed, and besides, what was the point of being worshipped if you didn't use it to your advantage? She would reward the devotion and prayers of the faithful and visit them in the morning.

Christou, their leader, was a desperate, needful little mammal, digging her up from the darkness as though fate had intervened. He was someone who wanted to have faith in something and she was in a position to reward any belief that came her way. So, she had appeared to him in the form of his dead woman, seductive and captivating, and used his grief against him. A little promise of immortality and he was hers to do whatever she wanted. Yes, she had plans for her prophet.

But, first, sleep and dreams of tomorrow's meal.

TWENTY-THREE

War woke. He'd fallen asleep in the chair at Elizabeth's bedside, still clutching his sword. As he shifted uncomfortably, the needles of pain reminded him of his immense age. Two large eyes stared out from beneath the bed covers.

'Why didn't you wake me?' he asked, rubbing his own eyes. They felt as if two billiard balls had been inserted clumsily into his skull. 'I swore to protect you and I can't bloody well do that if I'm asleep on the job.'

I thought you should sleep. You were tired last night.

War scratched at the itch in the back of his head. He was disappointed she'd retreated into herself after the events of last night. Fighting his way out of the chair, he said, 'I can smell breakfast. May I offer you a lift, madam?' Elizabeth nodded regally, her nose high in the air. War reversed up to the side of the bed and she climbed onto his back.

Do the horsey noises, she commanded silently.

Conquest had ordered Mrs Burgess to take the morning off and so he, Death and Famine had taken it upon themselves to prepare the most important meal of the day. They had met their Waterloo. And they'd been at the actual Waterloo. Burnt toast

114

littered the floor, the scrambled eggs had formed into a perfect rubbery sphere, and nobody would take responsibility for the porridge caked on the ceiling. They all sat at the breakfast table, arms folded, a simmering tension filling the air along with the smoke.

'I have to go to work,' said Death.

'I'd get changed if I was you,' Conquest replied.

'Why?'

'You can't go ferrying souls to the Afterlife with runny egg all down your cloak. It'll create a terrible first impression.'

War burst through the door snorting and neighing like a prize stallion, with Elizabeth on his back. He trotted around the table, treading toast crumbs into the carpet, until she brought him to a halt and climbed onto a chair. Conquest forced a grin.

'Good morning.' Elizabeth gave a shy smile. War surveyed the damage laid out on the table in front of them.

'So this is breakfast, is it?'

'Yes,' Conquest replied. 'What would you like?'

'Any scrambled eggs?'

'Famine, could you cut War a slice?' Conquest asked without looking at him. War wrinkled his nose up in disgust.

'Perhaps I'll just have cereal.' He turned to Elizabeth. 'May I get you some porridge?' Elizabeth nodded and War went over to the sideboard to prepare their meals.

Conquest watched the two of them with amused curiosity. The Horsemen were incapable of having

115

children; at least, there'd never been a knock at the door from some long-lost son or daughter. They'd never have the connection of blood from blood, so he'd never seen War form such an attachment to a human. Of the four, he'd always been the one to regard them as an inconvenience. Death's sole reason for existing relied on them being around, they fed Famine, and Conquest simply wanted to be loved by them. But War didn't need them, except as cannon fodder.

Elizabeth was different and special, and whatever forced itself into the house the night before was evidence of that, but Conquest still felt that War would've cared for her, anyway. That's the thing with humans. You get close to them and then you find you can't let go. At least, now, they'd found out what had probably happened to the Fairchild boy. The creature must have him hidden somewhere. They would need to go looking, but Conquest was concerned about leaving Elizabeth in the house now it knew where she was.

'Perhaps you two should go out somewhere for the day,' he said when War had returned to the table. 'I don't think the thing from last night will attack in public.'

War looked down at Elizabeth. 'Is there anywhere you'd like to go?'

Zoo. I want to see a penguin.

'Penguins are rubbish.'

You asked me if there was anywhere I'd like to go. I've never been to the zoo.

'The zoo it is, then.'

Elizabeth squealed with delight. Conquest looked from her to War. She had told him without talking. A connection so natural that War didn't even think it was worth mentioning. He considered questioning them about it, but last night's event had obviously frightened Elizabeth, so he left it for the time being.

Mrs Burgess knocked and entered the room. She was pale, her smile weak. 'Good morning, gentlemen. Miss Elizabeth. The carpenter has arrived, and he's boarding up the window in the library.'

'Thank you, Mrs Burgess, but didn't I tell you to take the morning off?' Conquest asked.

'I couldn't sleep for the worry that Mr Famine might burn the house down,' she said, producing a dustpan and brush from nowhere and sweeping the crumbs away.

Famine shrugged, defeated. 'The woman's got a point.'

'And there's still so much to do before I leave tomorrow.' In all the violence and confusion of the past twelve hours, Conquest had forgotten about Mrs Burgess's resignation.

'Oh, you're still going through with that, are you?'

Mrs Burgess planted her hands on her hips. 'Well, between the British weather and the monsters in the library, I could see why you think I'd change my mind and want to stay.'

'To be fair, it was just a single monster and in all the years you've worked here that was the first one we've had,' replied Conquest. 'I'd say this was a pretty good working environment.'

'What about the time War unleashed the Kraken?' Death asked.

'We were on holiday. That doesn't count,' War said through a mouthful of porridge. Conquest moved around the table and took the dustpan and brush from Mrs Burgess.

'I'll tell you what,' he said, 'Famine and I need to go to Scotland Yard this morning and War and Elizabeth are visiting London Zoo. Why don't you go with them? Get yourself out of the house. War's paying.'

'I am?'

Mrs Burgess narrowed her eyes. 'Do they have penguins there?'

TWENTY-FOUR

Mrs Burgess, Elizabeth and War virtually had the whole of London Zoo to themselves. On entering, they headed straight to the penguin enclosure. The birds all seemed perfectly happy in the frozen conditions, diving into the pool, the low winter sun glinting off the sharp blue water; a mirror image of the sky.

After War spoke quietly with the zookeeper, Elizabeth could even feed them. She wrinkled her nose as she dangled the silver fish in front of them, giggling as they waddled up to her comically, snatched the food from her fingers and gobbled it down in one.

Elizabeth was having a wonderful time. Once the penguins finished feeding, she asked to see animals from the African continent, things she thought she would never come face-to-face with in her life. The camels looked less amused trudging around in the snow, but War couldn't remember seeing an amused camel before, so perhaps it had nothing to do with the weather.

Mrs Burgess walked behind, silently watching her two companions. They didn't say much, but the bond was obvious. The way they shared smiles, or the times Elizabeth reached for the reassurance of

War's hand when an animal ran towards the fence separating them.

Mrs Burgess often imagined how, if she'd been blessed with a daughter, she'd be like Elizabeth; strong, intelligent, feisty. They and Mr Burgess would spend the weekend visiting the sights of London, perhaps take lunch at the small cafe they liked on Baker Street, and return home to snuggle together in front of the fire. But life carried on, ignorant of hopes and wishes. Instead, here she was in the cold staring at a miserable camel with an orphan and a demon. Perhaps the new life waiting for her across the ocean would be more receptive to her dreams.

'What would you like to see next?' she asked. Elizabeth consulted the small map they were given at the entrance.

'Wolves.'

'And in which direction are they?' Elizabeth pointed along the path.

'Actually,' War said. 'I need to do something.' Mrs Burgess recognised distress pass across Elizabeth's face at the thought of her protector leaving her. 'I'll only be a few minutes,' he said, 'I'll meet you there.' With Elizabeth placated, they went their separate ways.

A gift shop was an uncomfortable place for a creature like War. It contained too many items that could be described as 'fluffy'. He was more at home with hard steel and polished armour but, while walking around the zoo, it had occurred to him that unless somebody did something about it, Elizabeth would not get any Christmas presents. So, here he was, browsing shelves filled with cuddly toys and playthings; some related to the zoological theme and others less so. He stopped by a bucket of wooden swords and tried one out. It was never too early to learn the Mugai-ryu technique of the Samurai. War stepped back into a stuffed gorilla and, fearing he was under attack, turned around and tried to throttle it.

'Can I help you, sir?' the shopkeeper asked. War struggled to put the gorilla back into an upright position.

'Oh, I'm looking for a gift.'

'Well, you've certainly come to the right place,' the shopkeeper replied with a patient smile. 'Who is the gift for?'

'A young girl. Eight years old. My... err... niece.'

'And what does she like?'

War shrugged. 'She's a girl. Girl things.'

'The young ladies of today have many varied interests. Is she outdoorsy? Or, perhaps she enjoys more refined pursuits?'

War snapped his fingers. 'She likes gambling.' The shopkeeper's reaction showed War this wasn't the way to go. Then he saw something Elizabeth might like. A bright red chestnut stuffed horse about the size of a small dog. He stroked its dark mane. 'She like ponies.'

'An excellent choice, sir. Would you like it gift-wrapped?'

'Yes, please. The last time I tried wrapping a present I ended up gluing my beard to a war hammer.'

Unsure what to do with this information, the shopkeeper said, 'Will you be taking this with you now?'

War produced a wad of notes from his pocket. 'It's a surprise. I'd like to arrange delivery.'

War found Elizabeth kneeling in front of a cage, staring blankly at a wolf on the other side of the bars. He was old, with a grey beard hanging below its fierce mouth, and he was big; the leader of the pack. If it wasn't for the thick steel bars separating them, he could easily pick her up in his powerful jaws and crush every bone in her body. Greybeard returned her gaze. An alien anxiety knotted in War's stomach. Worry.

'What's going on?' he whispered.

Elizabeth said nothing, lost in the wolf's eyes. Mrs Burgess, standing over her with a look of concern, replied, 'She's been like that since we got here.' War crouched down next to Elizabeth, keeping the wolf in the corner of his eye.

'Elizabeth?' he asked in a hushed voice. She turned slowly, a distance in her eyes.

'He's sad,' she said in a faraway voice. 'They all are.'

'Who?' War asked.

She nodded at the wolf. 'The animals.'

'How do you know?'

'He told me. He wants to run in the forest, to hunt, not sit in a cage and be fed like a pup.'

War understood this. He was a kindred spirit. A creature as magnificent as Greybeard shouldn't be imprisoned by concrete and steel. 'What did you tell him?'

Members of the pack had come out of hiding behind Greybeard, padding listlessly around the enclosure like prisoners in an exercise yard.

'I said I would help. I'll help them all.'

'How are you going to do that? Start a petition?'

Elizabeth said nothing, but placed her hand on one of the cage's bars.

'No!' War hissed, afraid of startling the wild animal sat three feet away. The wolf remained motionless.

A loud click echoed around the park. The sound of thousands of locks releasing simultaneously. The cage door swung open. Greybeard, leading the rest of his pack, walked out onto the path and calmly wandered off around the corner. A pleasant family day out.

The other animals were far less composed. A tremor rose through War's legs and, as it grew stronger, into his chest. Elephants, giraffes, coyotes and beasts from every continent running for freedom. They smashed through walls, pulled trees down and tore up flowerbeds.

'Run!' War yelled. He scooped Elizabeth up in one arm and, throwing good manners away, grabbed Mrs Burgess's hand. They sprinted away from the stampede, but were too slow. Surrounded by teeth and claws, they were knocked from side to side, choking on dirt and snow.

When he noticed they were keeping pace with a lion, War knew they needed to escape the melee before they were dragged under and crushed. He glanced behind. A horse was coming up on their left. You could always rely on them as a species. When it drew level, War reached out and grabbed its mane. With one powerful arm, he leaped and swung his legs over the horse's back, wedging Elizabeth in front of him. Mrs Burgess stumbled and, just before she was smashed by hooves, War snatched her up and deposited her behind him. He kicked the horse's flanks, and she galloped forward.

War felt a rush; the raw animal urge for freedom thick in the surrounding air. He threw his head back and laughed, deeply and joyously.

TWENTY-FIVE

Inspector Graves of Scotland Yard had been a copper for over twenty years. He was married to the Force; faithful and committed to the Metropolitan Police, not like the other detectives who claimed they were married to the Force because the long hours and their questionable hygiene standards prevented them from finding a wife. It was in his blood. His grandfather had been a Bow Street Runner, his father one of the original constables when Sir Robert Peel had first set up the Met.

He'd seen many strange things in those two decades; the case of the Balham Petticoat Sniffer, the Stoke Newington Inexplicable Odour Mystery and the Gerbil-Faced Man of Camden Town to name just three. But none were as perplexing as the case he was now working on.

His investigations had uncovered at least six children snatched from their beds in the last fortnight, but none of them were as high profile as Douglas Fairchild. Nothing connected them to each other, other than the details of their disappearance, and the only clue so far was the small Christmas decoration found in the Fairchild boy's bedroom. Another odd aspect was the two gentlemen sat opposite him in his small office. The Conway chap seemed smart enough and Hungerford was friendly, even though he was eating fish and chips from newspaper at this time of the morning.

He'd tried to dig up information on the Gentlemen of Dubious Activities. They had the ear of the Prime Minister, so they were obviously powerful. He'd discovered that there were two more of them, but everything else was classified. Graves had made a career out of sticking his nose where it wasn't wanted, but his detection skills had been thwarted by the smoke and mirrors of government. And, as many people residing at Her Majesty's pleasure had learned to their cost, if Inspector Graves didn't know something, he wasn't happy.

'We have a lead,' Conquest said.

'What is it?' asked Graves.

'Too early to say at the moment. We'd like to do a little more investigation.' Inspector Graves was growing less happy by the minute, but had been given his orders.

'Right you are, sir.'

'Did anything come from following Mr Christou yesterday?' Conquest asked. Graves pushed a piece of paper through a maze of case files piled on his desk, the place where paperwork came to die.

'Constable Parsons has made a full report.'

Conquest ignored the paper. 'Tell me.'

'Archibald Christou left the Whitechapel building site at six o'clock in the evening and proceeded immediately to his registered address. He did not leave the property until eight o'clock this morning when he proceeded back to the Whitechapel build-ing site.'

'Well, that was a constructive use of time and re-sources,' Famine said, blowing on a hot chip and popping it in his mouth.

'There was one other thing,' Graves said. 'He was accompanied by a young woman.'

This shocked Conquest. Archibald never men-tioned there was a woman in his life. He wondered if she was what they euphemistically called 'a lady of the night'.

'Who?' he asked.

'I don't know, but we have a description.' Graves looked down at the report. 'Five feet five inches tall, mid-twenties, slim build, brunette hair. In fact, Par-sons is adamant...' He paused, unsure how to continue.

'Parsons is adamant about what?' Conquest asked.

'He's adamant it was his childhood sweetheart.'

'That's rather a coincidence.'

'It's less a coincidence and more like a bloody mir-acle,' replied Graves. 'His sweetheart, a woman by the name of Deidre O'Reilly, was fifty years old when she upped sticks and moved to New Zealand, where she died two years ago. Unless the air there is particularly rejuvenating, I don't think it's her.'

Conquest noted the doubt in Graves's tone. 'But?'

'I don't know, sir. Parsons is one of the most un-flappable men I have, but it shook him right up. Like he'd seen a ghost. He's convinced it was her.'

'I have no doubt he thinks that.'

'Any other questions?'

Famine looked up from his chips. 'Do you have any salt on you?'

'I'm very sorry, sir, I don't,' Graves answered drily. 'It's always the same when I leave the house. I always forget something. Keys, wallet, warrant card, various seasonings.'

'There's no need to be sarcastic,' said Famine.

'There's every need to be sarcastic, sir. I've got children taken by their dead parents, people driven mad by the sight of something unspeakable and now there's wealthy industrialists wandering around with antipodean ghosts. With the greatest of respect, what the bloody hell is going on?'

Conquest was formulating a reply when he was stopped by a commotion outside the office. There was a sharp rap on the door and a red-faced sergeant poked his head round.

'I'm sorry to interrupt you, sir,' he said, 'but we have a problem.'

'What is it, Jenkins?' Graves asked impatiently.

'There's been a breakout...'

Graves jumped to his feet. 'From the Scrubs?'

'No, sir. The zoo.'

'London Zoo?'

No, Edinburgh Zoo, Jenkins thought. *The zebras had read good reviews for The Realm of Joy at the Royalty Theatre and they all got the East Coast Mainline to see if they could get tickets.*

'Yes, sir,' he replied. Conquest closed his eyes and swore very, very quietly. Jenkins consulted a scrap of paper in his hand.

'So far, we've got an elephant on Wardour Street, a cackle of hyenas in Trafalgar Square and some penguins have taken over a pond in Regent's Park.'

'Oh, I love penguins!' cried Famine. He turned to Conquest. 'Can we see them?'

'A what of hyenas?' Graves asked.

'A cackle, sir. I believe that's the correct nomenclature. Davies looked it up in one of his books.'

'Thank you, Charles Darwin. What do you want me to do about it?'

'It's all hands to the pump, sir. The Chief Constable has ordered you to Westminster. There's a gang of apes throwing faeces at each other in the House of Lords.'

'Well, that's the upper classes for you,' replied Graves. 'Present company excepted, of course.' Conquest waved the comment away.

'Not a problem, Graves. You'd better get down there.'

'Thank you, sir,' Graves said, putting on his coat and hat. 'Excuse me, gentlemen. The case notes are on the desk if you'd like to read them.' Graves followed Sergeant Jenkins out the room, slamming the door behind him.

Conquest and Famine stared at each other in the silence. Conquest let out a short sigh.

'War. You can't take him anywhere.'

TWENTY-SIX

A dozen former members of the Righteous Order of Armageddon had assembled in the crypt below Christou House. Candles cast ghoulish shadows against the rough stone walls as they shifted uneasily in the uncomfortable wooden chairs arranged in a circle.

'What do you think he wants?' asked Lesley Atkins, a nervous, shrew-like man with small, sharp movements.

'How should I know?' replied Thomas Braddick. He'd joined the Righteous Order because he'd been told great things about Christou's wine cellar, but had converted to a true believer by his powerful arguments about the wretchedness of the world. Come for the Bordeaux, stay for the Apocalypse. Jeremy Rochester waved a hand towards the candles scattered around the floor. He spoke in clipped tones.

'He likes to put on a show, doesn't he?'

After they'd summoned the Four Horsemen of the Apocalypse and had been persuaded by them that destroying the planet might not be in everybody's best interests, they closed the Righteous Order. The group had tried to reinvent themselves, to find something to fill the time that had once been taken up by incantations and buying ceremonial candles. They'd tried jam-making and had performed charity work. They'd briefly formed an Association Football team, but it had all seemed too much like hard work and none of them saw the sport catching on. Nothing, it seemed, could fill the void left by abandoning their faith.

Recently, though, they'd all noticed a strange new energy filling the city. Something powerful had forced itself into their world. Lesley Atkins was the first to raise it in conversation during rehearsals for their amateur production of Much Ado About Nothing. Then Archibald Christou - a fine religious leader but poor goalkeeper - made an announcement. He'd had a revelation deep in the tunnels of his new underground transport system.

Esuries. A visitor from another world. A paradise unbound by such concepts as time and space. She was weak, but faith in her would help her grow strong. And when she was powerful enough, their worlds could become one. They would not destroy this world, but build a better one. A heaven on Earth where time was immaterial and nobody would die. The classical scholars among them were concerned the English translation of the word Esuries was 'the hunger', but Christou explained that this had come from the Ancients' desire for spiritual sustenance. Well, that had been fine by the Righteous Order. They packed away the sugar thermometers and jam jars, took down the set dressing and returned to a spiritual life. London was their church, the park lawns their prayer mats and the seats on the omni-buses their pews.

The fire of virtuous belief surged through them when they communed with the spirit of Esuries and they were filled with a euphoria previously un-known to them. Perhaps they were here in this low, cold room because the time had come. Perhaps their prayer and conviction had worked. Which is more than could be said for all the other sad religions.

The door to the crypt opened with a long creak. It's the traditional way for all crypt doors to open and Archibald Christou was nothing if not a tradi-tionalist. The conversation petered out as he descended the rough steps and took his place in the centre of the circle. He turned slowly, looking each member of his flock squarely in the eyes. He smiled, beatific yet triumphant.

'Gentlemen. She is risen.' A murmur ran around the circle. Archibald allowed himself a moment to revel in their wonder before turning and signalling to someone in the corner of the room.

Thirteen pairs of eyes saw thirteen different fig-ures step from the shadows. Esuries slinked and limped and stomped and moved in almost a dozen other ways. Some of the men fell to their knees, oth-ers wept and mouthed prayers of thanks. She joined Archibald in the circle and, when she smiled at him with Sarah's lips, Archibald's heart cracked a frac-tion more. When order had been restored, she addressed the group, and each heard a different voice.

'I thank you for your faith. It humbles one even as old as I. We stand on the threshold of a new dawn; a paradise where time will not concern you and death will not stalk the ones you hold dear. This world is my world and will be yours to share. I will bring this to you, but I must ask you for one more act of love.'

'Anything,' whispered Lesley Atkins, his eyes wet and heavy with tears. When he spoke, it was to his childhood friend who'd died at a tragically young age. 'Your will is our command.' The group were unanimous in their agreement. Esuries replied with a smile.

'I must regain my strength, but there are those that are trying to stop me from doing that. Some gentlemen have stolen something precious that I need to fulfil my promise to you and they are not willing to give it up easily.'

Jeremy Rochester stood up. 'Tell us who these heretics are,' he said to his first-born son who'd died in his arms aged five. Archibald nervously cleared his throat.

'The Four Horsemen.'

Jeremy sat down again heavily.

'Is this some kind of joke?' Thomas Braddick asked.

'This is some kind of test,' Esuries corrected. 'Unless you are not ready for such responsibility?'

Thomas bowed his head. 'Of course I'm ready. My apologies.' Jeremy stood up again. He was feeling light-headed.

'What have they taken from you? Some ancient relic? A mystical artefact?'

'A child,' Esuries said with a hint of a smile. Thomas closed his eyes.

'Oh, God. Is it too late to go back to the jam-making?'

TWENTY-SEVEN

'They're not natural.' A drunken Count De La Croix leaned unsteadily against the ornate drawing room mantelpiece. He hadn't stopped drinking since that morning on the duelling ground. Isabella, his wife, had confined herself to the east wing of the house whilst he found comfort at the bottom of a bottle, playing the duel over again and again in his head, the images blurring more on each repetition. Each shot he knocked back was an attempt to quench the hot stabs of shame. It wasn't simply the manner of his humiliation, it was the perpetrator.

William Conway was an industrialist who had the temerity to work hard; a self-made man who didn't even have the decency nor dignity to inherit his wealth. He'd taken it upon himself to claim equality with his betters and this would not stand. The class hierarchy had worked well enough for thousands of years and De La Croix would be damned if it would crumble while he had a say about things. What would be next? The working classes putting their grubby feet up on the chairs in the House of Lords? Women being allowed to vote? He shuddered at the prospect.

Having gathered his closest friends to join him in his descent into the mad darkness, they drank and complained about the state of the world with howls of impotent rage against the changes in society they were increasingly powerless to halt.

Once again, the conversation had turned to Conway. De La Croix waved a half-empty brandy bottle at the equally-inebriated crowd collapsed on the floor and over furniture.

'I shot and stabbed him again and again and he kept getting up as if he'd just woken from a nap. I heard the next day he was dining with the Prime Minister. And that's not to mention the flaming sword his companion was carrying.'

The Earl of Aylesbury sloshed red wine over the rim of his glass onto a Persian rug and slurred, 'What do you think he is?' De La Croix squinted and looked one of the two Earls he could see in the eyes.

'He's a demon, not of this Earth. Witchcraft, or its like, is the only explanation why a man of his poor calibre could rise so high so quick.'

Nathaniel Darcy laughed a loud, mocking bark. 'I've seen your shooting and swordplay. Perhaps you missed him and only made a mess of his winter coat.'

De La Croix stumbled forward. The brandy bottle slipped from his fingers and exploded in the fireplace, a full stop to the conversations in the room. Grabbing Darcy by the scruff of the neck, their faces so close they smelled each other's hot, stale breath, he spoke slowly in the silence.

'I stared into his eyes and I saw no soul there.' He released Darcy from his grip and looked around for a fresh bottle. William Quill-Couche poured himself a large scotch, most of which went into the glass. He swigged away, soaking his luxurious moustache.

'What can we do? We can't have demons running around the West End. It lowers the tone.'

'Is that a giraffe eating your weeping willow?' asked a drunken gentleman looking out of the bay window. De La Croix smiled crookedly.

'We should deal with him and his friends the traditional way, as our forefathers did with sorcerers, witches and heathen monsters.' Quill-Couche helped himself to a tray of olives.

'Ah, excellent. I enjoy a good lynching. One usually has to go to the countryside for that.'

TWENTY-EIGHT

Conquest rubbed his eyes roughly with the palms of his hands and let out a long sigh that had built up over millennia. He was tired of playing the father figure of the group.

'I never thought I'd have to say this, but you shouldn't go releasing all the animals in a zoo.'

War, Elizabeth and Mrs Burgess were sitting shame-faced on the sofa in the drawing room. Conquest rested an arm on a Ming vase, one of many priceless artefacts that decorated the room. There were sculptures from Ancient Rome, a Ngombe Ngolu ceremonial sword from the Congo, fertility symbols from deep within the Amazon rainforest. A first draft of a cross-eyed Mona Lisa hung on the wall, with eyes that followed you around the room whether you wanted them to or not.

'I'm sorry,' Elizabeth said, staring at her shoes. 'I couldn't help it. I was just sad they were all locked up like that so I wished they were all free and then they were.' Conquest saw the tears welling up in her eyes. He'd charged down bloodthirsty Mongol hordes single-handedly, but there was nothing more terrifying than a little girl about to cry. He smiled patiently.

'I know, Elizabeth. You have a good heart.'

'There's a monkey at the window,' Death said from an 18th Century leather wingback chair. Two large eyes buried in grey fur stared at them through the glass.

'I think it's a lemur,' said Famine.

'I thought a lemur was a monkey?' War said. Conquest put his head in his hands. Sometimes the other Horsemen had so little focus, such that if they actually tried to end the world they'd likely spend most of the time arguing over the difference between an Apocalypse and an Armageddon.

'I think the issue is that there are several hundred animals that are not indigenous to these islands running around London, which means the police are held up trying to recapture kangaroos, tigers and monkeys rather than helping us.'

'I told you, it's not a monkey.'

'Poor thing,' Mrs Burgess said. 'Maybe we should leave a mince pie out for it?'

'Go home, Mrs Burgess,' Conquest sighed. 'You're leaving tomorrow and you should be with your husband. I shall hail you a carriage.'

'There are mince pies?' asked Famine.

'If you say so, Mr Conquest,' Mrs Burgess said. 'And, yes, Mr Famine. There are mince pies. I've put them in a tin in the cupboard nearest the kitchen door. The one with all the teaspoons.'

She gathered her coat and bag. Conquest escorted her to the front door. Before he opened it, he handed her an envelope taken from his jacket's inside pocket. 'A Christmas bonus.'

'Thank you, sir.'

'We'll all be there at the railway station tomorrow to say goodbye.'

'That will be lovely,' said Mrs Burgess. Conquest nodded and opened the door. Beelzebub was stood on the doorstep, the collar of his fur coat pulled up around his ears.

'Did you know you have a monkey in your front garden?' he asked.

'It's a lemur, actually,' said Conquest.

'Is it for sale? A few of them and I could create a marvellous winter coat.'

'What do you want?'

'I can't pay a social visit to my oldest friends at Christmas?'

'I wouldn't call us friends. Former work colleagues, perhaps.'

'I'll be off now,' Mrs Burgess said. She was unaware of Beelzebub's true identity, but always felt uneasy around him, as if he was after something of value from her.

'Of course. Let's get you a cab,' Conquest said to her. To Beelzebub he said, 'Go inside. The others are in the drawing room.'

Beelzebub strode into the drawing room as if he owned it, which – to be fair – is how he strode into all rooms.

'Gentlemen!' he exclaimed, his arms held wide. 'How the devil are you?'

'Oh, bloody hell,' muttered War.

'War, my friend. You look great, not a day over five thousand years old. Famine! Have you lost weight? Death! You were always my favourite!'

Death waved lazily from his chair. 'What do you want?'

'A drink would be nice,' Beelzebub replied, heading towards the drinks cabinet. Noticing Elizabeth out of the corner of his eye, he stopped and jabbed a perfectly-manicured finger in her direction. 'She's new. Don't tell me you've employed child labour? The old lady not cutting it anymore?'

'She's the daughter of a friend of ours,' Conquest said from the doorway. Beelzebub spun round, a glint in his eye.

'Telling untruths to the King of Lies? Poor form, Conquest.' He turned back to Elizabeth. 'And who are you, my dear?' He felt a thrill of excitement run through his body as he passed through her field of power. A sly smile played at the corner of his lips. 'Oh, don't worry. I know what you are.'

Beelzebub was about as welcome in Conquest's home as forty thousand wasps in a well-tailored suit, but Conquest prided himself on being a good host.

'What can we do for you?' he asked. Beelzebub slipped his coat off and tossed it to War.

'Do something with that, will you?' He crossed to the drinks cabinet. A globe made of finest walnut. 'Very tasteful. I'm guessing this was your choice, Conquest? All the lands you've yet to wield your power over?' He tipped the northern hemisphere back, revealing an array of bottles.

141

'The bauble you showed me,' he said as he poured himself a generous measure of scotch.

'You showed him the bauble?' War asked in horror as he dropped the coat in a pile behind the sofa. Conquest nodded and signalled for Beelzebub to continue.

'It came from a child's bedroom. A child who was apparently abducted by his late father, whose death he never got over.'

'How did you know?' asked Conquest, trying to keep his poker face. Beelzebub sipped from the heavy lead crystal and smacked his lips.

'This is rather good, lads. Perhaps you have some taste after all.'

'How did you know?' Conquest repeated with more force than he intended.

'I am legion blah-blah-blah. You're not the only one with contacts. Also, your friend Christou was seen accompanied by something that looked like the witness's lost love. And I hear you had an unspeakable horror in here last night, and I'm not talking about War's underwear. I assume it's taken an interest in this young child. You are a special young thing, aren't you?'

'Her name is Elizabeth,' Famine said, irritated. 'And what's your point?'

'Do you have any snacks?'

'Yes, some mince pies,' said Death.

'Aces!'

'What's your point?' Famine pressed.

'What creature takes the form of your greatest desire and feeds on the souls of children who are, shall we say, gifted?' Beelzebub looked at their blank faces. Sometimes their ignorance astounded him.

'Esuries,' he told them.

'Esuries?' War repeated back.

'A powerful demon from a dark dimension.'

'Bollocks,' said Famine.

'There are children present,' War warned.

'Sorry.'

'And why are you helping us?' asked Death.

'As I told Conquest, it's purely self-interest. Esuries existed in a time of gods and demons. There was a natural order. Those balances disappeared when humanity walked away from them. Now she is the top predator crawling out from prehistory and she will devour the world in her ancient jaws. I cannot let that happen. I have tickets for the theatre next week.'

'Can you tell us where this Esuries might be?' asked Conquest.

Beelzebub stared at his drink as if he hoped the answer might be hiding in there. 'No, not yet.'

Conquest was tired and frustrated. He was about to make a flippant remark when a strange orange glow filled the window as if the sunrise had come early. War went to investigate.

'What is it?' Conquest asked him.

'Flaming torches,' War replied, peering through the curtains. 'Pitchforks. Standard angry mob.' Conquest's irritation grew. It never rained, but it poured. Torch-bearing, pitchfork-wielding angry mobs were an occupational hazard when you were an immortal creature not of this world. The timing of this one,

though, was less than ideal. He cracked his knuck-
les.

'Let's see what they want, shall we?'

TWENTY-NINE

Archibald Christou and the hastily christened Church of the Light of the Second Coming of Esuries gathered outside 84 McHoan Gardens. They agreed that the title needed editing at some point, but it just didn't feel official until they'd come up with a name. Cloaked and hooded, they had equipped themselves with whatever weapons they were able to lay their hands on at short notice; pitchforks, shovels, muskets, swords and hammers. The flaming torches flickered in the December air, stirring the shadows cast long against the orange-tinted snow. Esuries had charged them with a holy quest. Their former friends inside the house held the key to humanity's future and, for selfish reasons known only to themselves, they were unwilling to give her up for the good of mankind.

The anger rose in Archibald, climbing his spine, setting it like steel. He straightened up, shoulders back, finding strength of purpose. His grip tightened around the torch. The moment was close at hand. A prelude to battle.

'The children are the chosen ones. The first, envoys, pioneers,' Archibald told the crowd. 'Nobody will age, or die, nor be ravaged by disease like those we have lost. We will lead them into the light. This will not be our legacy, nor their inheritance, for we will always be together.'

The front door opened, and Conquest was silhouetted against the rectangle of light. He'd pulled a heavy coat over his loungewear and a hat over his head, adding bulk to his frame. He crossed the pavement, the snow crunching under the heels of his boots, and faced the crowd. One man against an army.

'Good evening, gentlemen.' His voice dripped with menace. The shadows carved dark lines into his face. For the first time, Archibald saw how ancient Conquest was. Even in a woolly bobble hat, the Horseman was an awe-inspiring figure. Archibald's resolve wobbled until he remembered the prize that awaited. He took an unsteady step forward.

'Give us the girl,' he said in a faltering voice.

'I'm afraid I can't do that, Archibald,' Conquest replied in a reasonable tone. Archibald hesitated for a moment, shaken at how Conquest had seen through the anonymity of his hood.

'Then we must go through you and take her.' He was surprised how easily the words came to him.

'I don't know what Esuries has told you, but no good can come of this.'

'She has promised us immortality. Why would you keep from us all you have yourself?'

Conquest looked to the sky as if speaking to the stars themselves.

'Immortality isn't all it's cracked up to be.'

Archibald held his hand out. 'Give us the child and nobody will ever die again. No more mourning, no grief, no-one will have to go through what I have. Help us.'

'And while those are noble reasons, I'm sure she's lying to you.'

Archibald snatched his hand back.

'Blasphemy.' He spat the word like poison from his lips.

'She appears as whatever you most desire, yet never fulfils what she has promised. Her life is nothing but deceit. Why would that change now?'

'That's not true!' Archibald screeched. Conquest folded his arms and cocked his head, inquisitive. An amused smile.

'How so?'

'She has given me that which she promised,' Archibald said.

'And what was that?'

'She promised that she would lay me with...' Archibald hesitated. These things should never be spoken in public, but he could not let Conquest's heresy go unchallenged. 'That we would make love.' The mob shifted uneasily behind him. Conquest's face was a picture of disgust.

'You slept with that thing? I mean, each to their own, but I'm just trying to think of the logistics. Where would the tentacles go?'

'She came to me in the form of Sarah.'

'Oh!' cried the other members of the church, a mixture of relief and realisation. Conquest mulled the details over before reaching a conclusion.

'No, that's still creepy.'

While everyone tried to put the image of Archibald and Esuries out of their minds, eight points of light appeared at the end of the road to their left. All eyes turned towards them. To be honest, Archibald was glad of the distraction. They grew brighter, floating and bobbing in the air, illuminating the surrounding buildings in a serene glowing bubble.

'They're torches,' a voice said from behind Archibald.

Soon the figures holding them were visible in the dancing light. Archibald's blood ran cold when he saw the tips of swords poking from the bottom of expensive winter coats. Did the Horsemen have supporters? Had they come to defend them? He could feel the nervousness of his men grow. Feet shuffled as they retreated from the light, breaking ranks.

'Who goes there?' Archibald shouted. The newcomers halted and talked amongst themselves. They, too, seemed confused. After a moment, the leader approached alone. The stranger's hood obscured his face, hiding his intentions, but Archibald noticed his hand rested on the hilt of his sword. You could cut the tension with a knife and serve it with custard. With his free hand, the stranger pushed his hood back.

'It is I, Lord De La Croix. Who asks?' Archibald was relieved. He should've had faith, for he was doing good work and would be protected. He'd heard of the events on the Heath and knew De La Croix was no ally of Conquest. Mirroring De La Croix's actions, he removed his hood. The cold air struck him like a slap to the face. 'Archie!' De La Croix exclaimed, visibly relaxing. 'What the bloody hell are you doing here?' Archibald shrugged and then nodded towards Conquest.

'Oh, you know. A crusade.'

'Oh, that's good. I was saying to Isabella just the other day you should find a hobby. What are you crusading for?'

'They're standing between humanity and the gift of immortality.'

'Very philanthropic of you.' De La Croix pointed to the Church of the Light of the Second Coming of Esuries. 'These your fellow crusaders?'

'Yes. Lovely bunch of lads,' Archibald replied. 'What brings you to this part of town?'

De La Croix sighed. 'The usual. Dishonoured my name and my family.'

'That doesn't surprise me.'

De La Croix slapped his forehead as if he'd just remembered to put the bins out. 'Oh, and I nearly forgot. He and his minions are probably demons, so I've formed a mob to burn their house to the ground and run them out of town.'

'Me too!' said Archibald with a laugh.

De La Croix chuckled. 'Small world.'

'It certainly is.'

'You wait one hundred and fifty years for an angry mob and two turn up at the same time,' Conquest muttered to himself. He cleared his throat. 'Can we get on with this, please? I'm sure you've all got homes to get to, particularly with it being Christmas and everything.'

De La Croix turned to Archibald. 'Shall we join forces?'

'Seems like the polite thing to do.'

Famine appeared at the door. 'Is everything all right out there?' he called out.

Conquest turned back to the house. 'It's fine. Go back inside.'

Esuries attacked from the right, the impact sending Conquest flying. As he crashed into the hard-packed snow, he cursed himself for letting his guard down. He pulled himself to his knees, gasping and choking down air.

Wide-eyed, De La Croix stared in horror at the snarling, slobbering abomination stood before him. He tried to say something, but the words were beaten by the scream that got there first.

'Don't worry, she's with me,' Archibald reassured him. He stood aside and pointed towards the house. 'After you.' When his head and stomach had stopped spinning, De La Croix drew his sword. He'd found his voice.

'Attack!'

THIRTY

Conquest was up on his feet and charging towards De La Croix before even he realised. He tackled him hard, hitting at waist height. They crashed into a snow drift, a tiny blizzard thrown up into the air, and De La Croix's sword skittered across the ice, out of reach. The two of them wrestled clumsily, rolling and sliding until they looked like they'd been dusted in icing. Conquest found purchase and, pinning De La Croix to the ground, delivered a single punch to the head. De La Croix went limp beneath him.

Famine had stepped out of the house to face the oncoming hordes. *Or was it a crowd?*, he thought to himself. *At what point does a crowd become a horde?* he wondered as he casually sidestepped a lunging pitchfork. He grabbed the handle and tussled with his hooded attacker. Wrenching the pitchfork out of his hands, he swung out. The handle connected cleanly with the side of the attacker's head with a crack and he dropped in a crumpled heap.

'Get in the house,' Famine barked as Conquest scrambled behind him. They squeezed through the entrance together as the crowd (or possibly horde) reached them, slamming the front door and pushing its bolts home.

Beelzebub ambled into the hallway. 'How'd it go?' Conquest and Famine leaned their full weight against the door, its hinges complaining about the repeated attempts of those trying to break in.

'Oh, you know how it is,' Conquest panted. 'We agreed to disagree.' The door's wood splintered, sending chips of paint flying.

'A little help would be nice,' Famine yelled over the sound of the impacts.

Beelzebub sipped his drink. 'How rude of me.' He turned back to the drawing room. 'Death! War! Could you come out here, please, and give Famine and Conquest a hand?' Death, War and Elizabeth sprinted into the hallway.

'Making friends again, Conquest?' Death asked.

'It's Archibald. He's in league with Esuries and he's after Elizabeth,' Conquest said, pushing his shoulder against the splitting door frame.

War opened a cupboard filled with an arsenal of weaponry and rubbed his hands together. 'Right. Who wants what?'

'No killing,' ordered Conquest.

'You're no fun anymore,' War grumbled. The smashing of broken glass silenced him. They were coming through the drawing room window.

'This house will end up looking like a glazier's dream,' muttered Death.

War selected a cricket bat, tried a few practice swings and strode towards the drawing room. When the first intruder appeared at the doorway, he swung as if hitting a six at Lord's, his actions sharp and precise. The intruder span round and fell into the path of those following him. He glanced back as the trespassers awkwardly climbed over the prone body. His expression was dark, a feral intensity in his eyes. He lashed out behind him, knocking another enemy to the ground. The movements were instinctive; this is what he was born to do.

'What are you still doing here, Elizabeth?' he snarled. 'Hide!' Elizabeth had only seen one thing more terrifying than War at that moment, and it was waiting outside. She ran deeper into the house, the sounds of violence receding. She climbed the stairs, attempting two at a time, but she was too small and stumbled. Laying there, she gasped as her little lungs tried to cope with the fear and exertion.

A small voice in her head ordered her to get up. Clambering to her feet, she continued to the first-floor landing. The noise below was closer now, the shouting and crashing louder. She headed to the back of the house, to her bedroom. She slammed the door behind her and leaned against it. Through the wood, she could feel the house tremble from the beatings it received.

The walls of the room closed in as if the house was a wounded animal crouching into a ball to protect itself. It was a figment of her imagination, but she needed to get out. Her sixth sense told her there was burning in its future. She'd heard too many stories about fires in locked sweat shops to know she didn't want to be in here when that happened. Her breath came in ragged gasps.

Elizabeth ran to the window, pushed it open and let the cool, gentle wind caress her face. She climbed onto the window's ledge and, looking down into the darkness, let herself drop onto the flat roof of the house's extension below. Her hands sank into the untouched snow as she steadied herself. Her fingers red and raw, she buried them under her arms as she scurried to the edge of the building. Wishing she'd stopped to get her gloves, Elizabeth gripped the drainpipe and, half-falling, half-climbing, reached the lawn below. She wiped her watering eyes with the back of a frozen hand. The cold was freezing up her thoughts, so only one word made itself bold and plain in her mind.

Hide.

THIRTY-ONE

De La Croix had woken up, found his sword, and staggered into the house, leaving Archibald and Esuries alone on the street. Esuries, looking like Sarah, was still dressed only in a silk wedding dress but didn't feel the cold. She could, however, feel Archibald's lust, and had already slapped his hands away several times. Human males were twelve gallons of hormones and fluids stuffed into a ten-gallon body-shaped sack. It was a wonder how they kept their minds on the job long enough to make it to the top of the food chain. Must be down to the women.

They listened to the sounds of destruction and injury drifting out through the broken windows. The curtains had already caught alight, the burnt fabric whipped by the wind, creating black snow that floated in the air.

'They're taking their time,' she muttered.

'It's the Four Horsemen of the Apocalypse they're fighting. They will not roll over easily,' Archibald explained. Esuries put her hands on her hips and sighed.

'If you want something done right, you have to do it yourself.' She hitched her voluminous skirt up and, despite Archibald's shouted objections, marched through the front door.

Elizabeth stood shivering in the middle of the lawn. She'd explored the garden thoroughly, leaving a circle of footprints spiralling in the snow, but the Four Horsemen were minimalists when it came to horticulture, leaving little in the way of vegetation or furniture to hide in or behind. She wondered whether it would be safe to go back into the house. All she wanted was for War to gather her in his arms and tell her everything would be all right.

The back door swung open, clattering on the brick wall and dislodging snow from the roof that slid onto the head of the cloaked man staggering out.

'Bloody maniacs, the lot of them,' Thomas Braddick murmured to himself. Elizabeth froze, exposed, with nowhere to run to. High brick walls trapped her on all sides of the garden. The man only had to look up, and she'd be caught.

He did.

'Well, well, well. What have we here?' Thomas asked, pushing his hood back to reveal a bruised and bloody face. His left eye had swollen and his nose looked as if it had moved slightly from the position where it had previously been located. He advanced towards Elizabeth. She stepped backwards, trying to keep the distance between the two of them, then slipped and tumbled onto her back, her arms and legs flailing and carving a snow angel around her. Thomas jumped on top of her, leering down.

'Looks like Esuries will have a new favourite now.'

Elizabeth heard a growl and a grey blur passed through the periphery of her vision. Then, just like that, Thomas disappeared from view. Screams and a tearing of fabric filled her ears. Elizabeth rolled over onto her side to see Thomas pinned to the ground by a large grey wolf trying to rip the clothes from his back.

'Get it off! Get it off!' he shrieked, trying to push the animal away. Elizabeth had only met one wolf in her life and she recognised him now.

'Hello, Greybeard,' she whispered, happy to see a friend. 'Probably best if you stop eating him.' Greybeard obediently dropped Thomas from his jaws and padded docilely over to Elizabeth. She sat up, wrapped her arms around him and buried her face in his warm, soft fur. Thomas was immediately up on his feet and running across the lawn, a ragged cloak flapping behind him, then he jumped onto a bench blanketed in snow and vaulted over the wall.

Greybeard watched Thomas before turning back to Elizabeth. He licked her face and checked she was unharmed. He was giving Thomas a head start. There was no sport in it otherwise. He tugged at Elizabeth's sleeve, pulling her unsteadily to her feet. When he was sure she could stand unaided, he licked the back of her hand and walked away, looking back to her one last time and bowing his head; a thank you.

And with two powerful leaps, he was gone.

Esuries stepped daintily over an unconscious worshipper blocking the entrance to the house, making sure her wedding shoes didn't get dirty. The wounded littered the hallway, groaning and clutching their injuries. Death, War, Famine and Beelzebub had surrounded those still able to stand. The fight was over; the invaders vanquished. To her right, the furniture in the drawing room had caught fire and Conquest was dragging choking bodies out of the smoke into the fresh air.

'Can I help you?' he asked Esuries. 'As you can see, we're not expecting guests.' Esuries smiled sweetly and punched Conquest, who hit the opposite wall, plaster crunching under the force of the impact. He slid to the floor. 'Can I get you a drink?' he asked, weakly.

'Where's the girl?' Esuries asked, advancing towards him. Conquest coughed, dust exploding into his face, and slowly pulled himself up, gripping the wall for support.

'You know what kids are like, she could be anywhere.'

Death, War, Famine and Beelzebub abandoned their prisoners, Death leading the charge. 'You dare do this in Death's house?' he asked in his scariest voice. Esuries grabbed Death by the throat and threw him back like a rag doll, knocking the others over like skittles. She turned to her men.

'Burn the place down. Smoke her out.' The remaining members of the Church of the Light of the Second Coming of Esuries nodded, fear etched into their faces, and ran off to find combustible items.

War stood up, dusted himself down. He rolled up his sleeves and walked towards Esuries.

'I make it a rule to never hit women. Or – well – a *thing* that looks like a woman.'

'Let me make it easier for you,' Esuries said, and turned into her true form. She picked up the three Horsemen and Beelzebub and tossed them all at Conquest, who'd just managed to stand unaided. They lay there, a tangle of arms and legs, as Esuries turned her back on them and ordered her men around.

Death could smell burning leather. 'Not the library,' he moaned as he imagined the centuries of knowledge being lost forever. Beelzebub was the first to his feet.

'Bugger this for a game of soldiers,' he muttered. Conquest pushed War's boot out of his face.

'What are you going to do?'

Beelzebub looked down at him, a mischievous grin on his lips. 'I'm going to save the world.' He paused. 'Now, there's a sentence I never thought I'd say.'

Beelzebub, in all his hellish glory, was a sight to drive a man insane. Horns grew from his forehead, stretching the skin which had turned the crimson of a dying star. His shoes slipped from his hoofs and the tail, swinging whip-like, tore through his trousers. By the time he'd reached Esuries, he'd grown over seven feet tall. He tapped her on what he assumed to be her shoulder. Surprised, she turned to see a demonic smile.

'I don't think we've been introduced,' he said before launching her through the wall separating the hallway and the library. The two of them fell through the newly-opened gap as brick and masonry rained down with a deafening crunch. Grappling amongst the burning books, they kicked up a fog of dust. Beelzebub was spat out through the hole and slid across the hall's polished floor, coming to a rest by the Horsemen.

'Oh, I've missed this,' he said with a chuckle, standing up and cleaning the dirt from his clothes. 'You have a lovely library,' he said, before correcting himself. 'Had... a lovely library.' He laughed maniacally as he charged back into battle. After a brief struggle, Beelzebub's head made a new hole in the wall.

'Well, are you going to find her or not?' he asked, before a tentacle wrapped itself around his neck and pulled him back through the hole. Conquest jumped up.

'Let's get on with it, then. We should split up.'

THIRTY-TWO

Sergeant Jenkins had found his calling when he joined the police force. He'd come for the beating of drunks, but - to his surprise - stayed to protect the community. What he hadn't signed on for was walking the streets looking for lemurs on a cold Christmas night.

'What even is a lemur?' he asked Davies who was walking alongside him.

'Some kind of monkey, I think,' Davies replied. They turned into McHoan Gardens in the rich part of town. There was some rowdiness at the end of the street; raised voices and people rolling around in the road. The smell of smoke in the air. Jenkins sighed. It was always the same this time of year. Parties getting out of control. People, especially the upper classes, couldn't take their drink. Still, at least it looked like he'd get a few beatings in.

'We should probably have a word with them, bringing down a nice neighbourhood like this,' Jenkins said as he drew his truncheon from his belt. Davies followed his lead and, slapping their truncheons in the palm of their hands, they marched towards the source of the disturbance.

'I've heard of you,' Esuries said as she slammed a heavy book into Beelzebub's face and he crashed into a nest of tables. 'Your worshippers wiped out legions of my own.' Beelzebub pulled a bookcase down on top of Esuries, weighty volumes bouncing off her leathery hide.

'Well, we get about,' he said. She shrugged the bookcase off her back.

'You and the others caused the death of thousands of gods and demons, selfishly taking and hoarding the faith we'd spent so much time and effort building for ourselves.' Esuries tossed a burning book at Beelzebub's head. It bounced off a horn, landing on the stairs the other side of the wall. Pages flew out and, caught by the heated air, drifted down onto the carpet, which ignited easily spreading crackling, spitting flames to the wood of the bannisters.

'You've got to keep with the times, give the public what they want,' Beelzebub said, rubbing his forehead. He ran at Esuries, keeping his centre of gravity low. Esuries scrabbled around for something to defend herself with, when her fingers wrapped around a thick book. She swung out.

The bible struck Beelzebub on the chin. The pain was excruciating as it travelled through his whole body, as if his blood was on fire. He crashed through the boards put in place of the broken windows. It was actually a relief when he hit the pavement, the snow cooling the firestorm coursing through his body. Esuries tossed the battered bible onto Beelzebub's chest and his agonies were reignited.

'Thank you for the advice,' she said, and left him writhing in the cold. Beelzebub tried to push the book off, but his fingers burned whenever he touched it.

Jenkins and Davies looked in horror at the devil himself. Weakened, he nodded to the bible on his chest.

'A little help, please?'

'I think we'd better get Inspector Graves,' Jenkins said in a high-pitched voice. Davies was already running down the road.

The fire had taken hold and Conquest knew his home was lost. The only thing he could do now was make sure everyone survived the night. Famine, War and Death searched the ground floor while he went upstairs. Several of Archibald's men had succumbed to the thick, acrid smoke and he carried them down the creaking stairs into the safety of the street.

Windows exploded, raining shards onto the street as they lay there, sprawled on the ground, choking down the night air to cool their burnt throats. The wind whipped smoke and sparks up into the black sky as Conquest charged back into the house. He wasn't going to stop until he'd checked every room. Taking the stairs two at a time, his foot punctured a weakened step halfway up. He pulled it free, tearing his trousers on a loose nail, and continued his ascent.

The smoke was too thick and he was forced to feel his way to Elizabeth's room. He tried the handle, but the door was shut fast. A well-placed kick to the lock soon fixed that. He ran to the room's open window, stubbing his toe on the bed, and stuck his head out, momentarily enjoying the frigid air. He wiped his eyes with a smoke-blackened hand. A small figure waved up at him and relief swelled in his chest.

'Elizabeth!' he called. 'Stay there! I'll come and get you!' Conquest pulled his head back inside, cracking the back of it on the window. The injury didn't slow him down and he ran to the stairs.

They shifted, and gave way beneath his feet with a loud crack. He fell almost the full height of the hall-way, landing in a bonfire made of the former staircase. He crawled out, stopping to put out a small fire in his lower back, and checked himself for injuries. Nothing except for a small cut just under his right eye.

'That was lucky,' he said to himself with a small chuckle.

Then the ceiling fell on him.

Elizabeth watched the flames through the windows and knew she wouldn't be able to make it through on her own, so she waited for rescue. A fierce heat radiated out, melting the snow under her feet and forcing her to retreat into the shadows away from the house.

The back door burst open, a tongue of flame rolling out and licking the wet grass. When the smoke cleared, War stood in the doorway. His beard was singed and his face blackened into a horror mask by ash and dust, but Elizabeth didn't care. He was exactly who she wanted to see.

They ran to each other, but Elizabeth realised her mistake too late. War's smile was all wrong. Crooked, as if crudely painted onto his dark smoke-mask.

Esuries snatched Elizabeth up in War's arms. Elizabeth struggled, kicking and biting like an animal caught in a trap, but Esuries was too strong.

'Oh my, you smell delicious,' she whispered into Elizabeth's cold ear. With one leap, Esuries cleared the wall and disappeared into the night, Elizabeth still fighting in her arms.

By the time the Four Horsemen found their way to the garden, Elizabeth's screams had faded into the distance.

THIRTY-THREE

The fire brigade arrived at 84 McHoan Gardens and did what they could, which was mostly smoke cigarettes and watch the house burn to the ground. The Horsemen picked through the smouldering carcass of their former home to find little had survived. So much history lost. They collapsed, exhausted and dejected, onto the kerb. Beelzebub left as soon as he was able, mumbling he had to 'see a man about a dog'.

Inspector Graves arrived with the mounted police, summoned by Sergeant Jenkins screaming about devils running through the streets of London. He quickly decided to arrest anyone he laid his hands on and sort it out down at the station.

'I sent men over to Christou's house, but they tell me it's deserted,' he said to the Horsemen. War lifted his head from his hands.

'We must find her.'

'We're doing all we can, Mr Warfield, but London's a big place and we have no leads.' This was War's first time handling grief. He passed through denial uneventfully, but had set up camp in the anger stage; an emotion he had a lot of experience with and could really get his teeth into. He jumped to his feet and grabbed Graves by the throat, lifting him up so he dangled in the air.

'That's not good enough,' he spat. Conquest placed a hand on War's shoulder.

'This won't help. Put the nice policeman down.'

War reluctantly obeyed. 'I'm sorry about that.' Graves loosened his collar and rubbed his red neck.

'It's all right, but you haven't explained who this girl is.'

'A family friend. We're quite fond of her,' Conquest replied.

'What does Christou want with her? What does he want with all those kids?'

Conquest looked at the others. War nodded a fatigued head.

'He's not responsible,' he said. 'A demon from another dimension has taken Elizabeth because it wants to feed on her psychic powers. We're worried that if it becomes strong enough, it will try to take over the Earth.'

Graves puffed his cheeks out and exhaled. 'The problem we've got is that my jurisdiction is limited to the boroughs of the Metropolitan district of London, which is in this dimension.'

'I assume you're not taking this seriously?'

Graves didn't need this. He should be on a train to his sister's where he planned to eat and drink her out of house and home. Instead, here he was dealing with four lunatics, with a whole load more of them down at the police station along with two bemused llamas and a python. Conway and Hungerford seemed relatively stable, but the one with the beard

167

was obviously as mad as a sack of badgers, and the bloke in the hooded dress scared the bejesus out of him. Given half a chance, he'd nick the whole bloody lot of them, but didn't want to explain that to the Prime Minister.

A young man dressed in the grey uniform of a courier company pulled up on a bicycle.

'Is this Number Eighty-Four?' he asked jovially.

'It was,' replied Conquest. The courier pulled a gift-wrapped toy horse from his satchel.

'I've got a package for a Mr Warfield?' War took the parcel from the courier and wandered off, leaving Conquest to sort out the tip. He handed over a few coins.

'I'm very sorry, but that's all I have. My house has just burned down, you see?'

'That's all right, sir. Happens a lot this time of year.' The courier tipped his hat and cycled off, the wheels skidding and slipping on the fresh ice.

War wandered away from the group, clutching the horse tightly, smearing the festive wrapping paper with his sooty fingers. He'd told Elizabeth he would protect her and had failed. The guilt sat heavily upon his chest; an open wound infecting him.

Help.

That itch in the back of his head again. The parcel slipped from his hand.

'Elizabeth?'

'Are you all right?' Famine asked War. War held a finger to his lips and everybody fell silent.

Help me, War. I'm scared.

'Where are you?' War asked the sky.

I don't know. It's dark and cold. Tears welled in War's eyes. He raised his fists to the heavens.

'I'll find you, Elizabeth,' he bellowed. 'I swear on my immortal life, I'll find you.'

You don't have to shout.

'Sorry.' War turned to the others. 'We must go at once.'

'Where?' asked Conquest.

War hesitated. 'I don't know.'

'Can I be of help?' Beelzebub had returned. With him was the most ferocious dog any of them had ever seen. Pitch-black, huge, with eyes that burned red with the fires of Hades. Beelzebub could barely keep the animal under control as it strained against the lead.

'I told you I was going to see a man about a dog,' he said, 'and here he is. This is Adrian. He's half Hell-Hound and half Rottweiler.'

'He's a crossbreed?' replied Conquest.

'He's a bloody angry breed, I know that. I call him a Rott-in-Hell.' The joke did not go down as well as Beelzebub had hoped.

'Who the hell is this?' asked Graves.

'I'm sorry,' said Conquest. 'Inspector Graves, this is Beelzebub, Lord of All Hell. Beelzebub, this is Inspector Graves.'

'Completely bloody doolally,' Graves muttered as he shook Beelzebub's hand.

'Why have you brought this thing here?' Conquest asked.

'A Hell-Hound can smell magic,' said Death.

169

'Correct. If that monster has left a trail of magic, Adrian here will sniff it out.' Beelzebub went to stroke the dog, but remembered he rather liked his fingers and backed off.

'Thank you,' Conquest said.

'You owe me.'

Back in charge, Conquest whirled round to face his men. 'Find what weapons you can.' The other Horsemen scrambled to their feet and searched through the masonry and rubble. Conquest turned to Graves. 'I must commandeer your men's horses.' Graves was happy to agree to whatever Conquest wanted if it got him out of his hair.

'We ride in five minutes!' Conquest shouted.

THIRTY-FOUR

Archibald staggered through the tunnel he had carved, the uneven surface making him stumble with nearly every step. The gas lamp bouncing and swinging in his hand cast dreadful shadows, distorting the rock, so it looked as though a hundred ghastly ogres accompanied them.

'Faster!' Esuries ordered. Elizabeth was unconscious in her arms, the dead weight impeding her progress and infuriating her as much as the puny human struggling to keep up. Eventually, they reached the crack in the world leading to the Other Place. Esuries lay her precious cargo in the cold mud while Archibald collapsed against the roughly-hewn wall.

'What now?' he asked between gulping breaths. Esuries smiled as Elizabeth stirred at her feet.

'We make the other gods jealous.'

'Now?'

'There's more than enough power in this girl to punch a hole between worlds, to pull one into the other. We will scour the Earth, scrub it clean and shape it in my home's image.'

Archibald pushed himself from the wall. 'You said nobody else would be harmed.'

Esuries patted her last follower on the shoulder. 'And they won't. Well, apart from the girl, obviously. What's the point of a world with nobody to rule? I will be worshipped forever with an immortal army to do my bidding.'

'You can't! You lied!'

Esuries cupped Archibald's head in her hand and stared deeply into his eyes. 'When did I lie to you? I promised you eternal life, and I will give it.'

'A life of servitude.' Esuries placed her hands on her hips.

'The glass is always half empty with you humans, isn't it?'

'I will not let you do this!' Archibald screamed, pounding her with weak fists. Esuries sighed and threw him into the stone wall as easily as swatting a bothersome fly. He crumpled to the ground, knocked out by the force of the blow.

Glad to have respite from Archibald's complaining, Esuries knelt over Elizabeth, who was laying on the threshold between the two worlds. She placed a hand on the child's forehead and a soft drone filled the tunnel, making the gravel and sand skitter and thrum across the ground. The hum increased in volume, turning the subterranean passage into a vast echo chamber, the vibration folding over itself like forged steel. Beneath Esuries, Elizabeth moaned as if troubled by a bad dream. The noise was now so loud it had developed its own weight, making the air thick and heavy. Esuries greedily drew on Elizabeth, the power flooding from one body to another. It threatened to overwhelm the creature, and she was forced to steady herself against the wall. Her head swam, the world pitched and yawed, but she focussed, channelled the energy where it needed to be, and soon something deep inside her gave way. A soft glow bled out from the fracture in the wall as her world woke from its interminable slumber.

A new dawn rising.

The breach widened, forced apart with a loud crack, and the wall fell away, boulders and sheets of rock crumbling and shattering. With a final tug, Esuries pulled her world across the breach. The Other Place spilled through the rift like oil; viscous and clinging, the rock scrubbing out whatever it touched. It slid over the gaslight, fossilising it beneath a colder universe, slithering beneath Archibald's still body, insinuating itself into the new world. It flowed impossibly upwards, climbing the walls, smearing itself along the ceiling that threatened to collapse under the tremors. Still the Other Place came, endless, like lava pumping from deep beneath the Earth, until it headed for the tunnel entrance, smothering and snuffing out each lamp lining the walls.

Elizabeth woke with a scream; not of pain but that of a child with something precious taken from her. She grasped Esuries's arm and her fingers burned the flesh beneath them. It was Esuries's turn to howl as she prised Elizabeth's grip from her, and then the howl turned to laughter. The pain was fleeting and came too late. The rebirth had begun.

An angry genesis.

A new world.

THIRTY-FIVE

The Four Horsemen featuring Beelzebub charged on horseback with apocalyptic fury. The Yuletide crowds dived for safety as they thundered through the city streets, kicking up a snowstorm in their wake. Adrian led the way, his tongue hanging from his vicious jaws. War had been the only one foolish enough to approach him with the bauble and he latched onto Esuries's scent, chasing it down.

Without warning, Death doubled over in agony, almost tumbling from his horse.

'What's wrong?' yelled Conquest, the wind whipping the question away.

'I don't know,' Death groaned. 'It's everywhere, like the whole world itself is dying. Or it's heartburn. It's sometimes hard to tell when you get to my age.'

'Do you want to stop?' Death looked at War, the cuddly toy stuffed into the knapsack over his shoulders. He straightened up in his saddle, snapped the reins, urging his horse on.

'No.' The roads narrowed the further east they travelled, forcing them into single file, and when they arrived at the edges of Whitechapel, Conquest knew where they were heading. His hand instinctively dropped to his sword, assuring himself it was still there.

When they arrived at the entrance to Archibald's tunnel it resembled a moonscape. Dead grey rock filled the trench, smothering everything, spilling out over the sides, making its way along the High Road. The workers had fled, leaving the streets deserted. Even the winter birds fell silent as the cold, hard stone subsumed the skeletal trees.

The riders dismounted at the lip of the trench and drew their swords. With their scorched clothes and ash-smeared grimaces, they looked as if they had dragged themselves up from the depths of Hell itself to seek vengeance. Beelzebub turned to Adrian.

'Stay!' Adrian laid down, the snow hissing beneath his hell-spawned body, and licked his dirty paws.

'This looks like the place,' Conquest said.

'Shall I tell that Graves fellow?' Death asked.

'If you could, thanks,' Conquest replied. 'And don't just appear in front of him. You could give him a heart attack.'

Death vanished with a pop as the air rushed in to fill the vacuum he left behind.

'Should we wait for him?' Famine asked.

'Yes, you know what he gets like. He'll feel left out.'

'So does this make me an honorary Horseman?' asked Beelzebub.

'There's nothing honourable about you,' Conquest replied. Death appeared at Conquest's shoulder.

'All done. He seemed only slightly perturbed. Oh good. You didn't start without me.'

175

Now their number was complete, Conquest and the others climbed down the stone-encrusted stairs and ran across the trench floor towards the tunnel's mouth.

'Perhaps we should've brought some of those torches with us,' Famine said, staring into the dark hole that led underground. War pointed his sword at the darkness and it ignited in a burst of flame, illuminating their passage with an angry red glow. He marched towards the unknown and the others followed closely behind. The tunnel was wide enough for all five of them to walk abreast and marvel at the ingenuity of mankind. The white circle of the entrance receded behind them quickly as they descended below the ground.

'So they plan to run locomotives through here?' Famine asked in a hushed voice.

'Yes,' replied War. 'Elizabeth and I travelled on one the other day'

Conquest looked at him from the corner of his eye. 'You?'

War shrugged. 'She wanted to go on one. I wanted an easy life. They're very convenient.'

They continued to walk in silence, their footsteps echoing on the smooth grey floor. When a curve in the tunnel eclipsed the sun, leaving the flaming sword as the only source of light, all five gripped their weapons tighter. They knew what they were heading towards and, though nobody would admit it to each other, she made them nervous.

Then, in the distance, a child's scream. It was almost faint enough to be dismissed as a breeze, but it stirred the Horsemen. They put their apprehension aside and ran towards it.

THIRTY-SIX

Archibald's world swam and spun. His head was sore, heavy and fragile, as if split open and packed with shards of glass. Muffled sounds fogged his ears and when he opened his eyes, he was horrified to discover his vision was a dark grey blur. As his nerves woke up, the shock of cold stone beneath him focussed his thoughts and, as the initial panic subsided, he realised he was staring at the tunnel's ceiling. He twisted his battered body, relieved that all his limbs travelled with him, and pushed himself up onto his hands and knees. Bones creaked, but didn't give way, and he counted to three before looking up. Agony ran up and down his spine, he saw stars go supernova, and Archibald worried he would fall face first onto the hard stone. The nausea soon passed and he saw two bodies struggling in the glow of the Other Place.

Elizabeth squirmed beneath Esuries, trying to break free from her iron grip. Esuries held her down with her full weight, thinking how nobody ever mentioned how annoying creating a new world was.

With supreme effort, Archibald pulled himself to his feet and the world plunged and reeled around him, forcing him to stagger as if on the deck of a storm-tossed ship. He heard a scream, a raw throat-scraping howl of anger and betrayal, and realised it was him. He ran towards Esuries, thrown forward by the fury of the humiliation she had heaped upon him. With the Four Horsemen nowhere to be seen, it would be up to him to stop her. He jumped on her and --

Was laying on his back where he'd woken up a minute before. This time he was sure he'd cracked at least one rib. A sharp, stabbing pain pulsed with the rhythm of his laboured breath. The life ebbed from him. His body was getting cold, and he was heading towards an ethereal light. His time was up. This world had no use for him anymore.

Except, the ethereal light seemed to be heading towards him rather than the other way around. And he didn't expect so much bickering in the Great Beyond. Archibald pushed himself up on his elbows as the Four Horsemen ran around the corner accompanied by a friend.

'I'm just saying it would be a lot easier if you made a map of all the lines and gave them different colours--'

Conquest halted when he saw Esuries. Archibald had never seen the Horsemen look as furious as they did now. Esuries had burned their home to the ground and now they had come to seek retribution. She put Elizabeth down and turned her attention to the newcomers. Time held its breath as the adversaries stared each other down.

Esuries moved first, charging at her enemies, whipping tentacles and scattering them across the tunnel floor. She continued to pummel them, thinking that if these fools were the best humanity had to defend themselves, their domination would be even easier than she'd hoped. The sound of the violence was deafening, reverberating off the stone walls. Seizing her opportunity in all the confusion, Elizabeth jumped to her feet and, looking for somewhere to hide, ran into the Other Place.

The Horsemen and Beelzebub stabbed and slashed at Esuries's writhing limbs. She evaded them with ease. While blows struck, most missed, the blades sparking off the stone walls. When the swordsmen had overstretched themselves, that was when she attacked. Tentacles wrapped themselves around arms and legs like thick rope, allowing Esuries to drag and throw the assailants like dolls.

'Where's Elizabeth?' asked War as he flew over Archibald's head. Archibald pointed at the hole in the wall.

'She went through there.' War picked himself up and found his sword.

'Thank you.' He turned to the others. 'Lads, I'll get Elizabeth. You all right to deal with this on your own?'

'No problem. I think she's getting tired,' Conquest groaned as Esuries slammed him into the tunnel's ceiling.

'Excellent stuff,' War replied, and jumped into another dimension.

With its grey, featureless sky and time-gnarled trees, the Other Place reminded War of a Scandinavian forest. Permeated with memories of ancient mysteries; a home to prehistoric sacrifices and un-speakable rituals. Searching the patches of snow, he couldn't find any tracks that led to Elizabeth. He thought of their parlour games just a few days be-fore when she'd told him how good at hiding she was.

He walked deeper into the woods, calling her name, hoping for an answer that didn't come. War wondered if she was watching him, but was afraid to reveal herself, unsure whether he really was who he appeared to be.

'Elizabeth! It's really me!' he shouted at the trees. 'You like penguins and Three Card Monte! I'm read-ing Alice in Wonderland to you at bedtime, though frankly, I don't really understand what's going on in it.' War stopped and let out an exasperated groan. 'Fair enough. Have it your own way. I don't bloody care, I haven't got time for this. I've got pan-dimen-sional monsters to hit over the head.' He turned around and walked the way he came, and Elizabeth jumped out from behind a tree he'd already passed.

'Only the real War would get so grumpy so quickly,' she said with a grin. War ruffled her curls with a meaty paw.

'Excellent to see you. Let's get out of here.'

While Esuries grudgingly admired her foes' pig-headed refusal to back down, she'd grown rather bored with fighting. The child had escaped, and re-peatedly throwing her attackers to the ground was wasting valuable time. Conquest staggered uneasily

181

to his feet and waved his sword in Esuries's general direction.

'Come on,' he said with all the energy of a man who'd been repeatedly thrown to the ground. 'I'm just getting warmed up.' Esuries let out a frustrated sigh. Famine and Death were slowly climbing to their feet, but at least Beelzebub was flat on his back unable to do anything except moan. Though she'd had the upper hand so far, they'd inflicted serious injuries and she was growing weaker by the minute. This brawl had to be brought to a swift conclusion.

She brushed her tentacles across the floor, taking the Horsemen's feet out from under them, making them crash into each other. In one fluid motion, she completed the sweep and ran for the entrance to the Other Place. She pounded the low ceiling with powerful limbs and a fracture appeared, growing wider with every blow, running along the rock until it gave way. Tons of stone sheared off, filling the tunnel...

And sealing War and Elizabeth in with Esuries.

THIRTY-SEVEN

'Are we lost?' Elizabeth asked.

'Of course not. I know exactly where we are, I just don't know where we need to be,' replied War. War had tried to keep track of landmarks during his search for Elizabeth, but unfortunately, he wasn't the woodsman he thought he was. All trees and rocky outcrops looked the same to him and they soon walked around in circles.

After a while, they stumbled into a clearing. A cold wind blew through the surrounding pines, spinning the angels and globes hanging from the branches; a glittering perimeter of glass and ceramic encircling a hole large enough to accommodate a sleeping monster.

Elizabeth gasped as the ornaments danced, refracting the light and spraying the trees with rainbows. She carefully stepped around the edges of Esuries's nest, drawn to one particular trinket; a small red sphere. Stretching up on tiptoes, she teased it from the thin, grey branch and felt a shiver of electricity as it dropped into her palm.

'This is him,' she said. 'The boy from my dream. His name is Joseph.' War took his bauble from a pocket and handed it to Elizabeth. She weighed both as if considering their value. 'This one is empty.'

'Break it.' Elizabeth was baffled. Adults were usually there to stop you from destroying pretty things. In the distance, the sound of branches snapping like gunfire; something large and furious approaching at great speed.

'Break Joseph's bauble,' War said with urgency. Elizabeth acquiesced, balancing the red bauble on a flat rock, and bringing her boot down, smearing the grey stone with crushed glass.

Joseph, still in the nightgown he was snatched in, looked around the forest in confusion.

'Where am I?'

'That's all rather complicated,' War replied. He looked in the direction of the noise. Esuries was getting closer. He turned to Elizabeth.

'Can you find the others?' She nodded, a look of grim determination on her face.

War smiled proudly. 'Good girl.'

'I know you,' Joseph said, staring at Elizabeth. 'You were in my dreams.' War massaged his shoulder before drawing his sword.

'I'll be back.' He sprinted into the trees, wondering if life would be easier if he ran away from trouble just once instead of always charging headlong towards it.

Conquest, Famine and Death clawed desperately at the wall of rock, sloughing boulders and shards away with their bare hands. With monumental effort, Archibald picked himself up and helped them. Beelzebub was sat on the ground.

'Why doesn't Death just transport himself to the other side of the wall? He can go wherever he wants.'

'Well, yes, in *this* world,' Death answered as if he'd been asked the stupidest question ever.

'And why are you helping them?' Beelzebub asked Archibald. 'You burned their house down a few hours ago.'

Archibald stopped his painful labour. 'I was lied to. I wanted to believe something so much, I became blind to what was going on around me. For that I'm sorry. Please, Conquest, Death, Famine. Forgive me.' Conquest gave him an awkward smile familiar to every British person who has been apologised to.

'Well, you know, it's only stuff. Nobody got hurt.'

'Actually, a lot of people got hurt,' Famine corrected.

'We can deal with it after we've found War and Elizabeth,' Conquest said. 'Just don't do it again.'

Archibald turned to Beelzebub. 'The question is, why aren't you helping?'

Beelzebub shrugged. 'All we will find is an all-powerful monster standing over War's corpse. Personally, I'm happy with having a rest before we deal with that.'

Conquest threw a rock deep into the dark tunnel and yelled with frustration. 'This is taking too long. Aren't there any tools down here?'

Archibald thought for a moment. 'There might be some explosives further down. They were planning on blowing through into a new branch next week.'

The Horsemen shared glances. Death dropped the rock he was holding.

'Death like big boom.'

Elizabeth and Joseph pulled the ornaments from the trees and smashed them under stones and fists. Soon, the rocks around Esuries's nest were smeared with spectrums of bright colour. The other children joined in as they were released, happy to destroy their prisons. Douglas Fairchild was joined by Nancy Briggs, Siobhan McGuire, Christopher Pope and Paul Hardwick.

They continued until only one decoration was left; the one War had given to Elizabeth. Joseph picked up a fallen branch.

'Throw it!' he shouted, swinging the wood like a bat. Elizabeth tightened her grip around the globe and looked in the direction War had gone.

'No. I need it.' The mood darkened. Elizabeth walked out of the clearing and the others followed, heading towards the sound of the violence.

They found Esuries and War locked in battle. Fallen trees, chunks of bark and bits of Esuries scattered the ground where they fought. The contest had been mighty. War looked beaten, down on one knee, his sword driven into the ground. He was holding it for support. Esuries, too, was battle-scarred and breathing heavily. Pulling the sword from the dirt, War thought he might have one last attack left in him, and clumsily charged towards Esuries.

Without a word, the children fanned out until they circled the two warriors; seven points of a

Christmas star. Esuries drove War back into the ground and, this time, he didn't get up. His body went limp, and the sword slipped from his hand. War had finally been defeated. Esuries turned her attention to the children.

'What are you all doing up?' she asked. Elizabeth could feel her anger rising. This wasn't fair. War was the only adult who'd ever looked out for her. The anger continued to grow, spilling out of her body until it was the manifestation of every small defeat and tiny frustration she had experienced throughout her young life. When it enveloped the group, she felt the other children in her head just as she was in theirs.

'What are you doing?' asked Esuries and, for the first time, Elizabeth detected a note of worry. She wasn't the monster that haunted their nightmares anymore. The children all moved towards their former captor, united; a perfect circle of trust. With every step, their power intensified, crushing Esuries and forcing her to become ever smaller. Elizabeth knew how this ended. When they were only three paces apart, she held the bauble out in front of her.

Two paces.

'No!' Esuries shrieked. 'I won't be a prisoner again!'

One pace.

That wasn't her choice to make. And then, they were seven children clustered around a cheap Christmas knick-knack. Douglas prodded it with a finger.

'Is she in there?' Joseph plucked the bauble out of Elizabeth's hand and violently shook it.

'See how she likes it.'

'Stop that,' Elizabeth scolded, taking it back. Elizabeth ran over to where War lay. Cuts and bruises covered his face and his clothes were torn and blood-stained. His eyes were closed as if he was sleeping. She dropped to her knees and took his large, calloused hands, cold to the touch, in hers.

'Don't leave me,' she whispered as the others gathered around her like sombre mourners. 'I don't want to be on my own.'

War opened his eyes to find seven children's faces staring down at him. A loud explosion rumbled in the distance, making snow fall from the trees and the ground shake beneath him.

'I have a pounding headache. I suppose nobody has any aspirin?' Elizabeth laughed and shook her head. 'Where's Esuries?' he asked. Elizabeth held the bauble up. 'Superb. A taste of her own medicine.'

War heard his friends calling for him. 'No rest for the wicked,' he muttered before shouting out to them. With Elizabeth's help, he staggered to his feet. He didn't want them to find him on his back. The Horsemen broke through the foliage.

'Where's Esuries?' Conquest asked. Elizabeth displayed the bauble, proud of her new trophy. Conquest smiled. 'Well done.'

'You look like death,' said Famine, examining War's injuries.

'Hey!' said Death.

'Sorry. Figure of speech.'

War looked down at the blood covering his shirt. 'Don't worry, it's not all mine.'

Conquest did a headcount. 'Come on,' he said when he was satisfied there was nobody left behind, 'I suggest we get back to our own universe.'

THIRTY-EIGHT

Elizabeth led the group into the blinding light of day. The trench was crawling with policemen and Conquest spotted Inspector Graves marching over. He gently pushed Douglas towards the detective.

'Inspector, I'd like to introduce you to Douglas Fairchild.'

Graves nodded to the young boy. 'Master Fairchild, your mother will be thrilled to hear of your return.'

'Thank you, sir,' he mumbled. Graves signalled to the other officers, who swooped in to swaddle the children in blankets and take them away somewhere warm. When one tried to coax Elizabeth away, War laid a hand on his shoulder.

'She stays with me.' The officer quickly backed off and found something else to do.

'I must admit, I didn't think you had it in you,' Graves said with a smile. 'Now, who's getting bloody nicked for all this?'

Archibald stepped forward and waved before turning to Conquest. 'I need to pay for my crimes.'

Graves shrugged and slapped a pair of handcuffs around Archibald's wrists. 'That works for me. You'd better have a good lawyer.'

'Don't worry,' said Beelzebub. 'I know loads of them.'

'Some of my men will be over to debrief you shortly,' Graves said, then turned and frogmarched Archibald away. After a few steps, he stopped and faced the Four Horsemen. 'Thank you, gentlemen. London can sleep easy on this Christmas Eve knowing you're watching out for them.'

'Quite all right, Inspector,' Conquest replied. Graves stood to attention and then marched off to do his duty and have a nice hot cup of tea.

Famine looked at his watch. 'Mrs Burgess's train leaves in an hour. We'd better make our way to the station.'

'Yes,' said Conquest. Then, looking down at Elizabeth, 'and we need to figure out what we do with you.'

War pulled Elizabeth close. 'She stays with us.'

Conquest was about answer back when he heard his name being called. He looked around and saw Johnson, the Prime Minister's assistant, striding towards him with a small group of men dressed in tweed. He looked a lot more confident than the last time they'd met.

'Mr Conway!' he called again. 'I'm so glad I caught you.'

'Johnson? What on earth are you doing here? And who are these fellows?' Conquest asked, pointing at the tweedy gentlemen.

'They're top-level boffins. We're here on behalf of Her Majesty's Government. Now, if you could just hand over the girl and the demon, I'll be on my way.'

'We'll do what now?' Conquest asked, incredulous.

'Mr Zebub has been keeping me abreast of the situation over the last few days. Esuries and Elizabeth will be the two greatest weapons in the British Army's arsenal.' They all turned to Beelzebub. He shrugged and stood shoulder to shoulder with Johnson.

'I just can't help myself. If it's any consolation, I only did for the money.'

'We need to take them in for study. With their power, the British Empire will never fall. It's your patriotic duty to surrender them. If you don't, there's a chance they could fall into an enemy nation's hands,' Johnson said.

All around the trench's perimeter, red-jacketed soldiers appeared, rifles trained on the Four Horsemen. The policemen down below scattered out of range. Conquest smiled. This was just like old times.

'Can I consult with my colleagues?'

'Take your time,' Johnson replied.

'One moment.' The Four Horsemen huddled together, Elizabeth tucked in the middle. 'Does anybody have any ideas?' Conquest asked.

War was never one for thinking ahead. He was more a 'stab first, ask questions later' kind of creature, but a plan was forming. A wretched and heartbreaking one. 'Can you get me and Elizabeth out of here?'

Conquest scanned the lip of the trench. He counted around thirty troops. 'We've handled worse.'

War nodded, his mind made up. 'Meet us at Waterloo Bridge station.' The Horsemen broke their huddle and turned to Johnson.

'I'm afraid we will have to turn down your offer,' Conquest said. Johnson's face turned red with apoplectic fury.

'You're disobeying your government?'

'Yes,' said Conquest. 'Didn't I make that clear?'

War put his fingers in his mouth and whistled. The horse he'd ridden earlier obediently appeared and slid down the trench's steep side.

'Hold on tight,' War whispered to Elizabeth before snatching her up and barging into Johnson, sending him sprawling across the hard stone.

The three remaining Horsemen drew their swords and ran towards the confused troops, who began shooting aimlessly. Bullets rained down on the people trapped in the trench, whizzing past them and ricocheting off the rock. The boffins, Beelzebub and Johnson dived for cover behind large boulders, screaming for their men to cease fire.

Shielding Elizabeth with his body, War weaved his way towards his horse. He felt the bullets hit him, puncturing his flesh, but they didn't slow him down. When he was close enough, he grabbed the horse's reins, placed a foot in a stirrup and swung himself up onto the saddle. He steered the horse towards the nearest slope. When they were only a few feet from the base, Conquest realised they would never make it up the sharp incline.

Then, he felt a little jolt of electricity and the floor dropped away from the horse's hooves. He looked down to see a mischievous grin on Elizabeth's face. The Red Jackets scattered, confused, but nobody was more confused than the horse as he floated up the sides of the trench. When he reached street level, he was relieved to feel the pavement beneath his iron shoes and galloped away.

'Could you warn me the next time you plan on doing something like that?' War asked Elizabeth. 'I'm not a fan of flying.'

THIRTY-NINE

Elizabeth still in his arms, War dived into the crush at Waterloo Bridge Station, pushing against the tide of humanity that threatened to sweep him out of the building and wash up on the pavement. He fought his way to the departures board and, after locating the Burgess's train, put Elizabeth up on his shoulders and waded his way to the platforms.

The express to Southampton sat idling, puffs of steam belching into the cold air, as War ran alongside it, close to the platform's edge. The crowds soon parted when they saw a burnt, bloody maniac running towards them.

'There she is!' Elizabeth cried, tapping War on the head. War looked in the direction Elizabeth was pointing and saw Mr and Mrs Burgess waiting by one of the carriage doors.

'Mrs Burgess!' he called over the heads of the Christmas travellers. Mrs Burgess turned and waved as War barged through those too slow to move until he reached the couple. Elizabeth dropped to the ground and hugged her.

'You made it!' Mrs Burgess said warmly. 'Mr War, you remember my husband, Stephen?'

War shook his hand. 'Of course. How are you?'

'Well, sir,' Mr Burgess replied stiffly. Mrs Burgess looked War and Elizabeth up and down.

'What happened? You look positively dreadful.'

'A long story. One that means I'm afraid I must ask a favour of you,' War said. 'I'd like you to take Elizabeth.'

'What?' Mrs Burgess asked.

'What?' Elizabeth asked.

'What?' Conquest asked, who'd just arrived with Famine and an invisible Death.

'There will be powerful men after her if she stays here and I'm afraid I won't be able to keep her safe. I will pay for your passage and whatever expenses you may incur but please, help her.'

'We can't do that. This is all a bit sudden. What have you got yourselves into this time? She doesn't even have a change of clothes with her,' Mr Burgess said.

'I can arrange for whatever you need to be waiting for you in Southampton,' Conquest said.

'There's this,' Famine said, passing the gift-wrapped pony to War, who wiped a layer of dust from the wrapping paper and gave it to Elizabeth.

'Happy Christmas,' he said.

'Can we, Stephen? Can we take her with us?' Mrs Burgess asked.

'You're agreeing with him? Where's this girl even from?'

'She's an orphan and ever such a wonderful child.'

'You are good people and she's a good girl,' War said. 'This is your chance to have the family you've always wanted, to give a child a future.'

Mr Burgess looked to his wife. 'Is this really what you want?'

'More than anything.'

Mr Burgess, who was indeed a good man, sighed. 'Fine.'

Mrs Burgess threw her arms around him. 'Thank you, Stephen.'

'But I don't want to go. I want to stay here with War,' Elizabeth said on the brink of tears. War crouched down in front of her.

'I don't want you to go either, but I swore to protect you and this is the only way. I know how men like Johnson think. He will not stop until he finds you, and I cannot allow that to happen. A new life in a new country will make that impossible.'

'Will I see you again?'

War wiped a tear from Elizabeth's cheek. 'I can't say. If I know where you are, then that puts them one step closer to finding you.'

'All aboard!' shouted the train guard. War took Esuries's bauble from his pocket and placed it in her small hand.

'I need you to look after this. Can you do that?' Elizabeth nodded and put it in her pocket.

'It's time to go,' Mr Burgess said. Elizabeth walked over to Conquest and Famine, and shook their hands.

'Good luck, Elizabeth and bon voyage,' Conquest said.

'Thank you for everything,' she said.

'It's quite all right,' Famine said with a sad smile.

Death gave a thumbs-up seen only by her. She giggled quietly and then returned to War, who held a hand out.

'Goodbye.'

Elizabeth pushed his hand away and wrapped her arms around his neck. War closed his eyes and returned the hug.

'I won't forget you,' she whispered.

In a moment of weakness, War almost told her to forget what he'd said. He imagined raising her, teaching her, watching her turn into the great woman she could become. But, deep down, he knew it could never happen. She would be safe and happy far away from him and that was all that mattered.

'And I won't forget you, Elizabeth Burgess.'

Elizabeth let go of War and turned to Mrs Burgess. 'Is that my name now?'

'Yes, if you want it to be,' Mrs Burgess replied, tears streaming down her face.

'And you'll be mother and father?'

Mr Burgess cracked a smile. 'If you'll have us.' Elizabeth smiled. Lynne and Stephen enveloped her in a warm hug and it felt like home.

After they'd said their goodbyes, the Burgesses boarded the train. They took their seats and Elizabeth, clutching the toy horse in one arm, waved excitedly from the window. The guard blew his whistle, and the locomotive pulled out of the station carrying the new family off to the new world.

The Four Horsemen of the Apocalypse watched the train pull itself along the tracks until it rounded a bend and disappeared from view, only the plume of steam visible above the dark heart of the city. Conquest turned to War.

'Are you all right?'

He nodded. He was War. Horseman of the Apocalypse. Destroyer of Empires. 1874 Inaugural McHoan Gardens Hide-and-Seek Champion. He smiled.

'So, we're homeless and the government is after us. What do we do now?' asked Death.

Conquest shrugged. 'I don't know.'

'Well, it's Christmas,' Famine said. 'Does anybody fancy a drink?'

War put his arm around Famine's shoulder.

'That's the best idea you've had this century.'

BIG LIST OF AWESOME

For a fourth time, the publication of this book would not have been possible without the support and generosity of the following. They rock.

Christopher Love, Alison Jayne Rodwell, Luke Orchard, Kirsten Wilson, Mike Walker, Ryano, Ahnlak Revedemort, Kev White, Hilary Seymour, Mathew Smith, Richard Claydon, Mark Scorah, Matthew Sholar, Sarah Nottingham, Backstagebear, Andy Davies, Lee Rawlinson, Ann Winsper, Andy 'Troozers' Stewart, JimmyGulp, Chris King, Carl Potter, James Ronan, Bex Wallace, Dr Pam Lynch, Pamela Marrache, Jonathan, Matt 'My Inspiration' Spiceley, Westley Bone, Rossco, Suze O'Shea, Paul Laker, Dad, Rita, Dawn Friesen, Katya Whittaker, Federica De Dominicis, Catherine Donald, Vashti, David Stretch, Michael Ch'ng, netty, Ilona Stretch, Pierre L'Allier, Gizmo, Richard Glover, 'The' Julie Park, Ray Reynolds, Howard Fein, Chris Basler, Anthony Williams, Shaddow, Sean Morris, Kylie Rixon, Garrick Baker, Richard Bairwell, Steve "Marvin" Holden, Graeme McAllister, James Wilson, Darren Jalland, Andrew Manning, Matthew Searle, Debs Nock, Neal Bailey, Tim Campbell, Michael Hallard, Elizabeth Hirst,

Paula Bailey, Matthias Werner, Andy Silvester, Robert, JanCherryJovi, Richard Mole, Emma Treby, Sarah Munn, Ida Wood, Steve Hine, Jayne Rowe, Sarah Netherton, Gareth Hopgood, Jennifer McDannell, Jonathan Caddy, Rob Sked, Toby Nutter, Bryan Poor, Tracy & Wez Fisher, Josepha Kalsbeek, Julian Tabel, David Patterson, Katy Heaton, Andy Payton, Corina Lalonde, Vincent Whittaker, Steve Nixon, Karl & Kate Hadfield, Stephen Clarke, Aaron Weight, Ian Davidson, Kate Davie, Ryan Williams, Christina Evans, Greg Tausch, Tracy & Tavish Clement, Robert Ryan, Adam Maxwell, Alex van Niel, Tomáš Slapnička, Thom Willis, Delwynne Cuttilan, Anthony Brown, tech-no-logical, Jane, Tim, William and Ruari Bardell, Ronda Snow, Luke Burstow, Nicola Leaning, Bob Pack, Eoin "Gogz" O'Neill, Jennie Webb, Catherine Britt, Christopher Booth, Jay Freeborn, Lindsay Ashford, Lisa Frankland, Graham Nealon, Emma Garner, Emma Louise Wright, Lord Lenny Jarvill, Lorraine Hatchwell, Sarah Woodhouse, Matt Haswell, Spencer Schill, Karen Blanden, Chris Bartram, James Lelyveld, Alexander Gräfe, Liam Mulvey, Julia Johnson, Nick Tan, Timothy Griffin, Steve The Destroyer, Jim Harker, Karen Hancock, Lidbert, Dave Wilkinson, Mariyah Mokhtar, Laura Chapman, Linda Mussoline, WSC, Neil Quinn @zirconencrusted, Bob Hamers, Ben Jones's Daddy: Mick, Neil Thurlow, Saz, Meghan Jones, Joanne Ahern, John Prow, Mighty Sprog, James Mead, W.A. Brown and Malcolm Chapman.

Printed in Great Britain
by Amazon

47612763R00118